For my family,
with love

and with thanks to everyone
who made music with me during my year

Agenda

Prelude

When you discover a new interest in middle age, there are two ways of dealing with it. One, you spend five minutes fretting over the fact it's eluded you for so long, but then adopt a 'better late than never' approach and rejoice in the prospect of weekends on the golf course. Or two, you stamp your feet and throw in your reliable nine to five existence, confident that the world is poised and ready to pay good money for your contribution to flamenco dancing.

My reaction is to steer a middle course between these two extremes, and the bet-hedging doesn't stop there. Which new interest am I talking about, as they're multiple? Ever ambitious, I hope I can combine them, whilst maintaining the security of a part-time job in university administration. Preferably without jeopardising my role as domestic lynchpin. Multi-tasking, here we come.

Music takes centre stage, of course, as you will have gathered from the title. Just before the turn of the millennium, a large regional choir welcomed a less-than-confident soprano into its ranks and she's never looked back. It comes naturally to write of that version of myself in the third person, such has been the transforming effect of choral music. It even inspired me to take up the piano again at the ripe old age of forty-six, having been uninspired by my childhood lessons – new interest number two.

Number three fights its way to the surface a couple of years later, when I summon up the courage to enrol for a long-threatened creative writing course. So many words, so many ways to manipulate, tease, cajole them into a unique form of self-expression. And yet so little time. My tutors – bless 'em – quickly tuned in to my natural inclination to write about all things musical, whether in fiction, travel-writing or journalism, and thankfully awarded the academic equivalent of a standing ovation.

After poring over notes of every type, this book is my way of indulging in all my creative pursuits at once, a reprise of the trials, treats, tribulations and triumphs of a year of living musically.

September
Sink or swim

My year doesn't start on 1st January, ushered in on the downbeat of some bizarre New Year's resolution. Nor can it strictly be confined to a finite twelve-month period, blurring rather into a continuous way of life. But as significant moments go, being persuaded to allow myself to be elected as choir Chairman has to rate quite highly, so let's begin there.

I'd joined the management committee four years earlier, propelled into direct involvement by the motivation of experiencing our first foreign exchange, singing with and enjoying the hospitality of a French choir in Orléans. There was no gentle easing into committee activity, though. All of a sudden, the Secretary's position unexpectedly became vacant, and in my naiveté I made the crucial error of quaveringly uttering the words 'I wouldn't mind doing a little bit of correspondence'. And the rest. I certainly chose an interesting time to take on this mammoth role, as, on top of the day-to-day administration of the choir, not only did I shoulder the minor inconvenience of finding seventy-five beds for returning French visitors but also the major responsibility of helping select a new Musical Director, or the MD as he shall henceforth be known.

When I was studying Spanish, shortly after the Inquisition, I read a wonderful, though tragic, novel called *El Jarama.* It concerned a group of teenagers on an outing to swim in the eponymous river (you can perhaps imagine what the tragedy turned out to be), watched over by a rather sinister character known only as *el hombre de los zapatos blancos* (the man in the white shoes). He remained nameless throughout, though after his introduction in full he was abbreviated to *el hombre de los z.b.* This kind of shorthand strikes me as very useful for my present purposes, where I sensitively need to ensure a little anonymity, so with apologies to Rafael Sánchez Ferlosio, I'm shamelessly stealing his idea. All the best composers did the same thing, you know. Most of the people to be encountered within these pages will quite neatly have a two-letter acronym applied to them, and after all, written music's basically a code, so hopefully you, dear reader, will soon catch on. There'll be more about shoe-colour too, no doubt, in musings about the thorny issue of concert dress as the year goes on.

My three-year stint as HS (Honorary Secretary) more than introduced me to the complexities of everything that goes on behind the scenes of a large amateur choir. And, believe me, it's complex. The prospect of a happy 'retirement' from all this organisational rigmarole happened to coincide with our return visit to France, where of course the fuse of my enthusiasm was re-lit. In fact, I can pinpoint the moment of truth. The MD singled me out immediately after one of our concerts to thank me privately for being the sole soprano to hold on one particular note in the ballad *Shenandoah* for its required dotted minim and a bit, to mangle the technical term. Not only was it flattering to be noticed and appreciated, but it struck me as forcibly as clashing cymbals that such perception and attention to detail was a compelling force to be reckoned with. Only afterwards did it occur to me that he'd applauded merely the duration of the note, so let's hope it was also the right pitch.

In any case, the result was that I realised I wouldn't be happy without continuing to contribute organisationally as well as chorally, so I volunteered to specialise in marketing and communications. Barely had I perfected the art of the persuasive press release and initiated some 21st century projects like e-newsletters, than the retiring Chairman asked if I'd consider taking over from him at the following Annual General Meeting. It wasn't the easiest decision to take, but I eventually agreed, despite – or actually because of – changes that were afoot in the realms of my 'proper job'. In a period of uncertainty, the choir was my one 'constant', aside from my family life. Not only did it offer me huge fulfilment, but I realised I still had plenty to give back and I could make a difference in doing so. So I decided to take the plunge. It turned out to be the deep end.

The weekend preceding that milestone, the AGM, I was lucky enough to be given a multitude of reminders of how vibrant and enriching live music can be. *Artsfest* turns the centre of Birmingham into culture heaven for a couple of days once a year. For free. Add to this some long-awaited warm, sunny weather, and the place was buzzing. Every possible taste was catered for in terms of visual and performing arts, both outdoors and in the city's municipal buildings. It presented the perfect excuse for my first visit to the Town Hall, whose associate performers were being showcased.

First on stage – actually, owning the stage – was female quintet *Black Voices*. Displaying a sense of innate rhythm so typical of black musicians, and unaccompanied close harmony that was effortless to listen to, they gave the foot-tapping audience a seductive selection of soul, spirituals and more besides. I feared for their voices in one number. No lyrics, but the ladies transformed themselves into a jazz band – bass, sax, flute, trumpet, trombone – not only in miming the respective players' actions on their imaginary instruments, but also in reproducing the sounds. Amazing.

No damage was apparently done to the vocal cords, though, as they continued with strong, confident voices, through which resonated the sheer joy of singing. Their broad white smiles were infectious. Clearly it was too important to keep to themselves, as they invited the crowd to join in with a civil rights anthem, having first taught us to master the correct rhythm for 'nah, na, na, na, nah ... freedom now!' Then back to simply entertaining with their remaining songs, a glorious expression of teamwork. As my neighbour – a total stranger prior to sharing this musical moment – remarked, 'Isn't the human voice a wonderful thing?'

Another visitor wasn't quite so absorbed by the musical experience as to pass up the opportunity to bemoan the subtlety of the recently refurbished Hall's décor. She would have preferred more glitz and glam. Following the crowd down from the balcony of the traditional shoe-box building, I took in the pale misty blue walls and roman blinds, the damask effect of the organ pipes in eau de nil, relieved by light touches of gold which echoed the huge sun motif on the ceiling. I found it classy indeed, and a lovely understated backdrop, which allowed the music to be the star of the show.

My next stop was CBSO Centre, practice venue of the City of Birmingham Symphony Orchestra, where an open rehearsal of the *City of Birmingham Young Voices* was in full swing. Swing being the operative word. No sheet music in sight; an extraordinary rapport between Musical Director and singers; a sense of controlled improvisation and above all a boundless enthusiasm for the act of making music. Again there was a 'freedom' theme – 'Freedom for South Africa ... see the kingdom come' – and whatever one's political persuasions it would be difficult to remain immune to the liberating influence of the music itself, so catchy were the rhythm and harmonies as delivered by the swaying, beaming singers.

One young man in a wheelchair wore a tee shirt bearing the legend 'My other body's a temple'. My friend, if you can sing like that and communicate such joy to your audience, your body's a temple anyway.

I called in at the Art Gallery, where a quartet of clarinets playing beneath fine English landscapes in the Round Room attracted quite a following. The audience amongst the display cases of the Industrial Gallery not so much listened to music as watched it, as the *Music in Motion* society interpreted songs in sign language, an experience both sensual and moving in every sense of the word. Doubtless invaluable for the hearing-impaired, but also adding an extra dimension for the listener, bringing the words to life.

Back at the Town Hall, by then it was standing room only to hear *Ex Cathedra*, accompanied by their junior choir. The children's lady conductor wore fabulous dressy black trousers with an extra filmy layer over them, which struck quite a contrast with the children's casual but colourful 'Sing Up!' tee shirts. While the main choir, up in the balcony at organ loft level, were put through their paces by their own conductor, the children sat quietly on the floor of the stage below. Children in the audience also sat on the floor in the aisles, the carnival atmosphere highlighted by balloons they'd acquired during the day.

Although some of the individual pieces from the classical choral repertoire were unfamiliar to me, it was so much the style that I enjoy both listening to and performing that, after the variety on offer all day, it felt like coming home. The quality was very engaging, from adults and children alike, and especially so when they performed together under the direction of both conductors on progressive stages. Through half-closed eyes, it created the illusion of double vision, but the sound was as clear as a mother's lullaby.

The children took us on a journey, with stunning diction in *America* from *West Side Story,* then some very clever dynamics and haunting melodies in an Aboriginal song *Bele Mama.* This required some preparatory shifting of music folders at their feet, the reason for which became apparent when the stamping choreography kicked in!

The adults continued the international theme with *El Ultimo Café,* a beautiful vocal tango. Secular was followed by sacred again, but still with a South American focus, as they sang *Dulce Jesús Mío* (Sweet Jesus Mine) whilst simultaneously processing down from the choir seats to take up positions along the side balconies. The children appeared cradled in between. Not only was the choir now closer to their audience, whether down below in the stalls or in the raked balcony, creating greater intimacy, but the music itself took on a different, more intense, quality. As *Ex Cathedra* worked together on Thomas Tallis' *Canon* across the expanse of building, you could identify the individual voices and yet it was still a coherent whole. And it was a tangible reminder, if any were needed, of the sheer power of live music.

Three weeks into the new term, the new choral year in fact, the choir sat expectantly in their new seats in a new rehearsal venue, ready to vote for their new Chairman. We even had a new piano! Would there be a sudden rush of opposition candidates, and would I find myself demanding a re-count, not to make sure I got in but just in case I could wriggle out of it? But the chances of a battle for this dubious position of power were as infinitesimal as a demisemiquaver. Played staccato. Rarely have I witnessed a group of a hundred people unanimously agreeing to something so readily. Would the applause, though, have turned into a slow handclap by the next AGM?

Thankfully that thought didn't linger, as, with the boring business safely and rapidly out of the way, we pressed on with the important stuff: the music. Our Christmas concerts would celebrate the life of Ralph Vaughan Williams, fifty years after his death, and his music required a lot of hard work – for reasons that would become apparent as the term wore on. So we quickly became absorbed in the *Fantasia on Christmas Carols.* In mid-September, this was slightly disconcerting, but then comfort and joy is at least more cheerful than gloom and despondency, and I can think of worse tunes to have buzzing around your head.

I was in good company taking on new responsibilities. The same week, Andris Nelsons officially became Music Director of the CBSO, and I had the pleasure not only of witnessing one of his first performances but also hearing him in pre-concert conversation with CBSO Chief Executive, Stephen Maddock. Andris' passion for that evening's orchestral music was touchingly evident, but it was also a revelation to hear about the great choral tradition of his native Latvia. I made a mental note to visit at festival time, when 30,000 singers apparently grace the stage at once! Or did the new Maestro's English (better than my non-existent Latvian, it goes without saying) unwittingly multiply the choir tenfold, perhaps? Whichever, he was a good ambassador for his homeland's love affair with music.

At a mere 29, he also had the enthusiasm of youth on his side. Whereas I felt rather as though I'd been handed the keys to the cupboard marked 'self-destruct button', unless I took a crash course in the art of delegation, Andris was described as having been given 'the keys to the toyshop' as he made himself at home in Symphony Hall. He displayed a thorough sensitivity to the Hall's outstanding acoustic possibilities, varying the apertures of the sound baffles for each of the three pieces and positioning instruments offstage as appropriate. Most spectacularly in Berlioz' *Symphonie Fantastique,* he stationed four separate timpanists up in the 'gods', perfecting the illusion of thunder rattling above and around the audience's heads – so much more effective than if they'd been on stage.

Andris spoke of another image he tried to evoke in the movement entitled *March to the Scaffold*, of the condemned man's stamping feet kicking up dust. It was doubtless just such perception, sensitivity and imagination which inspired the orchestra to a thrilling performance. You could tell they loved him already, and when asked what he thought of them, he replied that their success stemmed from putting the music first as a team. Team or no team, though, Andris, trying to get the band up on their feet to share the applause, was forced to acknowledge it for himself as the leader mischievously stayed put, tapping his bow on his music stand while the audience went wild and Andris humbly beamed.

Our choir had never been known as the most radical, but I decided to risk confiding to my new committee that, like violinist Tasmin Little, 'I like to do things differently'. Not that that would lead to us performing on oil rigs or in prisons (carefully avoiding the 'captive audience' joke), as per Tasmin's *Naked Violin* approach to broadening the appeal of music, but they might as well be forewarned that innovations were likely.

My first gathering with them, for example, wasn't so much a formal meeting as a post-rehearsal trip to the local pub. The Mermaid, it was called, which I found personally appropriate since I was at that time learning a Weber piece on the piano, *Song of the Mermaid*, to play as a duet with my teacher. It was a very simple melody so for once I stood a chance of keeping time with her, in the same vein as the teamwork of choral singing. Duets are a tremendous way of encouraging the hesitant to keep going despite mistakes, as you've got your partner to consider. As for any qualms about mistakes that lay in wait in managing the choir, luckily I had the calm support of a Vice Chairman, henceforth known as the VC, who would always help me think positively and put things in perspective.

Not to mention the MD's encouragement. Given that my opening gambit to the committee was an exhortation to focus on putting the music first in all our deliberations, it was a stroke of unwitting genius that during the preceding rehearsal he began to wax lyrical about how the way Vaughan Williams had constructed just one bar of the *Five Mystical Songs* made a particular musical point. Much of it went through our well-tuned ears and out the other side, I suspect, as it did get a bit technical. But the MD's passion for the music was palpable and spoke volumes about how enriching this wonderful thing called music can be for us as participants and, through us, for our audiences. The music itself transcends the notes on the page.

I was in the fortunate position, from working with and around the committee for several years, of knowing most aspects of its operation, and even more crucially, the personalities involved. Managing people in the workplace is one thing, but leading and inspiring a group who voluntarily give of their time and skills to get things done is quite another. I was all too aware how easy it would be to fall into the trap of flogging a willing horse, as it always seemed to be the busiest people who would shoulder yet more responsibility. I was determined to aim for the widest possible participation, in the hope that 'many hands make light work' would triumph over 'too many cooks spoil the broth'.

Let's go for a third proverb and wonder whether familiarity would breed contempt. I didn't think so in this case, as the team embarked on this new year from a standpoint of mutual trust and respect, mixed, no doubt, with some anticipation about how the new girl would shape up. They certainly felt comfortable enough with me already to make a mock show of choosing a seat for me. Would I be requiring a chair with arms, for example, to signify my importance? 'If anyone so much as considers calling me Madam Chairman ...,' I said, threateningly, at which point the MD addressed me as Madame Chairperson. To avoid any semblance of control dissolving altogether into the nearest pint, I quickly proposed a toast to the choir and to our music.

After a crescendo of clinking glasses, there was a long enough hush for me to make a little speech, assuring everyone of my commitment to the cause and setting out my expectations. I rounded it off with the hope that all choir members would become ambassadors, and strayed off-script to describe how I find that I'm at my most animated – and most infectiously enthusiastic – whenever I find an opportunity to talk about music, and especially about the choir.

One manifestation of my 'doing things differently' was an attempt at revolutionising committee meetings so that chat could be translated more easily into action. Therefore we didn't even have an agenda as such for this gathering, just a list of things to discuss – except that of course the HS pointed out that this was in fact an agenda. Whatever the terminology, once we'd dispensed with the most pressing planning issues, dealt with in efficient style by the Concert Manager (CM), namely the multifarious points leading up to our two Christmas concerts, we reached the item entitled 'Next term's exciting news'. I should have known better. This elicited cries of 'Congratulations!' and 'When's it due?'

The only birth, though, was of a little gang called the Go Betweens (GB), made up of a few representatives each from our choir and another local choir. They'd arranged to ponder the possibility of a joint concert the following Easter. Both choirs had planned to perform Haydn's *Creation*, just a week apart and at the same venue, and this was just the sort of unfortunate programming that could have a negative impact both on audience numbers and choir morale. It had already been discussed amicably and The Other Choir had graciously decided on an alternative work, allowing us to proceed with our plans for *Creation*. But when the grapevine leaked the news that The Other Choir's musical leadership was uncertain, it seemed like the perfect scenario in which to explore a mutually-beneficial collaboration. Not least, given a pooling of resources, we'd be able to better afford to secure the services of a good professional orchestra for the occasion.

I gave the committee a very brief overview of the situation, which, far from being my own initiative, was a legacy from the ex-Chairman (XC), who would help steer it by dint of being active in the GB. So the committee could digest it at their leisure, I gave them copies of an explanatory letter I'd written to our Vice Presidents (VPs) – a small group of members with vast past experience of running the choir, and who were occasionally called upon for advice in extraordinary situations – and didn't particularly invite comment, pending the first meeting of the GB. Stunned silence, on the other hand, was never likely, and sure enough, there was some initial reaction. Aside from the obvious question 'Would there be room for everyone?' I have to admit to being rather surprised how positively the committee received the news. So that first meeting, dabbling in the shallows with the mermaid, gave me a sense of confidence and optimism.

Within the week, this was to be coloured by a large dollop of frustration. Why did I have to have this thrown at me now, just when I thought I was about to set my own agenda (or 'list of things to do')? Not least, the choir was screaming out for younger voices but this had never really been tackled seriously. I was keen to try and capitalise on links with the music department of the university where I worked, and bang on cue, there was some interesting news via the online staff newsletter. My contact there, Kevin, had recently had the honour of taking a school choir to the World Choir Olympics in Austria, and was equally keen to foster links with other groups, so the possibility of working together seemed well worth exploring. However, the 'would we, wouldn't we?' debate about working with The Other Choir had to be dealt with first and took up swathes of time. The Go Betweens helpfully did the groundwork but their report needed to be digested and the salient points extracted so the committee could efficiently reach agreement about next steps. The report of their first meeting rang alarm bells for me as, reading between the lines, I sensed an inevitability not only about the joint concert but maybe even about a future all-out amalgamation. In my state of inexperience, this tested my position to the limits as I tussled with the helplessness of a perceived power shift. Perhaps openness isn't always the best form of defence but I voiced my insecurities, and received assurances that the decision-making process lay with the respective committees and that the GB merely acted as a broker. Marginally convinced, I valiantly pressed on.

Limited to barely a fifteen-minute interval within the rehearsal, I quickly fired my prepared bullet points at the committee and sought a consensus on whether or not to commit to the joint concert. We came up with some ground rules concerning finances and rehearsals, but the main sticking point remained whether or not we'd all fit into the desired concert venue. The MD suddenly had a brainwave and gave us visions of sections of the choir being stationed in the balcony if stage space didn't suffice. An interesting concept, about which there would prove to be varying views during the period of enforced waiting before the staging provider could measure up. A period of being on tenterhooks, you might say, conjuring up a picture of singers suspended from the balcony, perhaps.

Whatever my own hang-ups on whether or not this was the ideal way to start my career as Chairman, my predecessor had some very encouraging comments after the committee emerged from our interval huddle. He commended the unprecedented efficiency and claimed I'd soon be calling 'Time out!' in mid-rehearsal, gathering the committee for a 35-second conflab and returning having established a major new policy. I decided to take this at face value, as sarcasm really wasn't his style. And anyway, who cared if I ended up with a reputation for being bossy if it got the job done?

The real job was to get the music learned, however, and back in rehearsal we were treated to our next theory lesson. The MD found himself inspired to give us the low-down on modal harmonies, which began with a description of a piano keyboard. Oh dear, I thought, he's realised some of the other stuff went over our heads so now he's really going back to basics. But this was by way of preamble to a brief romp through the various types of scales, the variations hinging on where the semitones fall. Because Vaughan Williams favoured modal harmonies, with their particular pattern of tones and semitones, not based on the usual major and minor scales, this was a break from the tradition of his day, and resulted in intervals – distances between notes – that seem unexpected. Difficult and unnatural as they may seem, though, there's something very satisfying about labouring over a few solitary bars, chord by painstaking chord, striving for and appreciating the precise harmony that the composer intended.

October
The return of Little Red Hen

All of these little asides about the philosophical aspects of music struck a chord with me as they began to breathe life into the pages of Eric Taylor's indispensable theory books. I suppose I could call him ET, not after the Extra-Terrestrial, but in recognition of 'Equal Temperament', the 12-toned system of musical tuning which hinges on pairs of adjacent notes having identical frequency ratios. But why on earth would a grown woman want to learn music theory? After all, it's about as accessible as a cross between the fiddliest maths you can think of, physics (see above) and Greek. With an Italian accent. When I joined the choir, I knew the basics and could distinguish a crotchet from a crescendo. But as far as I was concerned, a slur was an insult on one's character, a tie was something gentlemen wore round their necks, triplets were siblings born on the same day and an accidental meant it wasn't a planned pregnancy. Unlike the outmoded dots and dashes of Morse code, though, in the age of the information superhighway, those on the music page continue to be the *lingua franca* between composer and exponent. Without wishing to reduce music to mere mechanics, if you want to tackle it properly, you have to know how it works.

Not only did I want to tackle it properly but, for reasons unfathomable even to myself, I wanted to leave my options open in case, in a fit of masochism, I decided to subject myself to further piano exams. My piano teacher (PT) agreed, without the most confident attack I've ever witnessed, that I was realistic in setting a target of the end of the academic year to achieve Grade 5 Theory. Achievable, measurable targets are good, and I'd proved equal to my previous one, Grade 5 Piano at

50.   I'd even written a thinly disguised semi-autobiographical short story about it, in advance of the fateful exam day, almost putting a jinx on it in the process. Never again, I'd said, and yet somehow I found myself learning the repertoire of Grade 6 scales and getting to grips with next year's Grade 6 pieces, which included a lovely number by Oscar Peterson. The fact that it was taken from his *Jazz Piano for the Young Pianist* appealed to my sense of irony.

Beyond Grade 5, though, pianists of whatever age are not permitted to venture without the corresponding theory certificate, and there was always that feeling of 'just in case …'

I wasn't trying to cram it all into one year, of course. I'd learned plenty of theory as I'd gone along but had never proved it formally – only casually to myself by doing exercises and practice papers from the earlier grades.   In some of the most unlikely places.   I'm possibly the only person ever to have sat by a French pool trying to overcome a mental block about time signatures.   So much for time being irrelevant on your holidays.   I'm not sure why it was always time signatures that got me confused, as did those exercises where you had to complete a rhythm based on an opening bar or so. These I always found particularly annoying because there was no melody involved, just a pattern of dots all on the same note, which struck me as a little tedious. (But then I'm a soprano, not an alto.) Vitally important, though, in giving the right structure to music. I was taught that in sight-reading tests the over-riding factor was the rhythm. Hitting the correct keys would be a bonus, too, of course, but this had less value than displaying a grasp of the music's shape.

I'd long harboured a fantasy that it would be fabulous to play percussion, but recognised that a more innate rhythmic ability than mine would be needed for a realistic assault on the battery. And I had to face facts: I was more of a words person. Rather than counting properly, I tended to rely on a sort of internal metronome and a decent aural memory.

But something of a breakthrough came with the application of this theoretical stuff to real music. Vaughan Williams had a field day with time signatures in the closing pages of his *Fantasia*. There we were, merrily singing about the new-born king in 9/4 time, dotted minims, duplets and *pocchettino animato* galore, when all of a sudden our three beats to a bar became two and we were faced with 6/4 time, whilst the baritone soloist wallowed underneath, blessing the ruler of the house in 2/2 time. This latter could have been written to match the choral lines, but by all accounts VW's approach saved ink! All we needed to remember was that each of our dotted minims was equal to one of the soloist's normal minims. Are you still with me? Then followed a brief foray into 9/4 again. And I mean brief: one bar. Followed by one bar of 6/4 (well, for the choir anyway; by this stage the soloist was back in 3/2, of course), another couple of bars of 9/4 then we were treated to some simple time, flitting between 3/2 and 2/2, interrupted for a few happy new year bars of compound 6/4 and ending with a breath-defying few bars of 3/1, where the ethereal *pianissimo* dotted breves, equivalent to three semibreves each, felt as though they'd go on for evermore, Amen. The result, assuming everyone watched the MD sufficiently to keep pace with these subtle changes (possibly a dangerous assumption), was music of a very interesting texture. A sort of controlled unpredictability – or predictably uncontrolled if we didn't watch. All this and tricky harmonies, too.

In the background, potential harmony between The Other Choir and us continued to demand the committee's attention. The GB had deliberated over the complexities of equitable financial commitment to the joint venture – the commitment being sizeable, bearing in mind professional soloists, orchestra and extra staging – and brought a fair proposal to the table at our next mid-rehearsal huddle. No problems there, then – or so we thought. Our MD felt he could live with The Other Choir's wish to hold independent rehearsals for the first half of term, so no problems there, either – or so we thought. The one remaining unknown was how to accommodate the combined choir in the church. With the site visit scheduled for the following day, the discussion was again full of conditionals and hypotheticals, and still featured the possibility of a balcony contingent. To my surprise, the committee didn't completely dismiss this as too divisive and difficult to manage as per their original reaction. Maybe it was seen as preferable to the GB's suggestion of wielding registers and bringing rehearsal attendance to bear in a bid to limit numbers participating in the concert if necessary. The choir had trodden that path before and it's one that leads to trouble!

Whichever way I looked at it, there was no getting away from the impression that everyone concerned was determined to make this happen, whatever it took, especially so that we could have our professional orchestra. Not that I was against the joint concert personally, indeed could foresee many benefits, but shouldn't I have felt more in control, less swept along with the tide? Was I ready for the responsibility, could I sufficiently stand up for my own views? Was I getting in too deep? Just as well the work in question wasn't Vaughan Williams' *A Sea Symphony*, or we'd be even more awash with watery metaphors, although there's plenty of H_2O in *The Creation,* of course.

Maybe I should have considered managing a children's choir instead. Tasmin Little certainly didn't seem to be fazed by surrounding herself with small people at an 'up close and personal' family session on a Saturday morning in Birmingham Town Hall. Leaving aside the trifling matter that she was wielding a violin rather than woodwind, she had the magnetism of a modern-day pied piper, but thankfully not the treachery. No intention of stringing them along to a nasty end, rather an early appreciation of how her beloved instrument worked and the magic that could be conjured from it. As with her groundbreaking interactive website, Tasmin's aim was to take the mystique out of classical music. It turned out she'd had an even more unusual, and potentially frightening, audience in the past, so maybe that explained why she made it look like child's play.

The children were invited to sit at Tasmin's feet, from where they were suitably relaxed to interact with her. Using a question and answer technique, interlaced with excerpts of music and flourishing scales to illustrate her points, she imparted a wealth of knowledge in child-friendly fashion but which was equally valuable to ignorant adults! We learned about everything from the instrument's origin and physical properties – acoustic chamber, sound post, 'f' holes, horsehair bow and a variety of mutes – to its tricks, Tasmin awarding her rapt audience special praise when they volunteered the correct Italian terms – *pizzicato* (including a fancy two-handed version), *tremolando, ponticello, glissando.* The audience participation didn't stop there, as not only did we have to sing 'Happy Birthday' to the 300-year-old Stradivarius, but the children helped act out the story of Ferdinand the Bull, narrated by Tasmin's actor father, George, while she played the recurring signature tunes of the various 'characters'. Unlike the other bulls, their aggression depicted by plenty of bouncing bow *(ricochet*

27

or *saltando)*, Ferdinand's theme was a gentle *legato* number because he just liked to 'sit under the cork tree and smell the flowers'.

One of the tiniest participants got her moment in the spotlight. With pigtails and a pink Winnie the Pooh jumper, she came complete with a quarter-sized violin that appeared to be a permanent extension of her arm. During the interval she gave a mini-recital to some of the other little girls, so Tasmin found herself re-entering the Hall to someone else's applause. 'Have I missed another concert?' she grinned. With admirable versatility, she capitalised on this and gave the pint-sized performer an opportunity to play to the whole crowd. Wearing the most serious of faces, five-year-old Adastra – how perceptive of her parents to give her a name meaning 'to the stars' – took the place by storm. 'You heard her here first!' said Tasmin.

She encouraged the children to ask questions, which ranged from 'Why do you have strings?' to 'Do your arms ache?' And then, from the same questioner, 'Do your fingers ache?' A budding physiotherapist, perhaps. The grown-ups were allowed to join in, and perhaps not surprisingly there was considerable interest in the optimum quantity of practice. Tasmin wisely skirted round this and advocated capturing children's enjoyment by giving them pieces that they like and want to be able to conquer. That way, practice becomes a pleasure rather than a chore.

My own question sought to understand a little more of this extraordinary woman. 'Where's the most unusual place you've performed?' I asked, feeling slightly conspicuous with my notebook in tow rather than a small child. Tasmin beamed, as though she'd been waiting for just this question. She launched into an animated anecdote, telling how she'd given a concert on the deck of a small boat on the Zambezi, with the audience on the riverbank. She played the Rondo from Bach's *Gavotte,* the very piece with which she'd opened our session. Gradually, she noticed the audience's attention wandering away from her, and wondered why. Following their gaze, her eyes alighted on the most enormous hippo in the water, just a few yards away from her. She carried on playing though, because of course hippos are vegetarian – and she's also a consummate professional. The hippo basked there, transfixed, for the entire eight minutes of the *Gavotte,* then calmly swam off, a happy hippo. Whoever said you shouldn't work with children and animals?

I wonder if whoever said that a camel must have been designed by committee ever negotiated between two committees at once? They would have loved that. You would have thought the GB's initial go-between phase had reached a happy conclusion when, hurrah, it was found that there was room on stage for all possible singers in the combined choir. Metaphorical green lights flashed in email boxes various, a formal invitation was issued to The Other Choir, a firm booking made with The Professional Orchestra. The formal response from The Other Choir, though, was 'wait a minute, someone's just come back from holiday and thinks we've got a poor financial deal, so watch this space.' Trying not to lose my patience altogether, I suppressed the secret hope that it would all fall through and we could go back to some sort of normality, while the GB battled it out some more. Up-front investment in the project was adjusted, but by the same token our choir would pocket all ticket income rather than carve it up. This meant we'd need to put the publicity machine into overdrive to ensure every seat had a backside on it, preferably a well-padded one, since the pews weren't famed for their comfort.

But it wasn't a deal-breaker, so the GB's hiccup was cured and I found myself in the joyous position of announcing the project to the general membership. If I ever put as much effort into learning the music as I did into this, I'd be note-perfect by now. I knew I'd have to forestall countless questions, demands, pleas for reassurance, so I prepared in minute detail. It would be wonderful to take this sort of thing in one's stride and deliver an off-the-cuff summary, but I stood there with my script, apologising for looking like Dixon of Dock Green reporting to the press pack outside the crime scene. The preparation paid off (as it would, no doubt, with the music) and they accepted it like lambs. I wasn't hoping for a mutiny, of course, but the lack of reaction left me with something that could best be described as an anti-climax. Definitely *not* to be mirrored in the music.

My own individual rather than collective brand of music continued to progress at the piano keyboard at a snail's pace. I've no idea how that particular tempo would translate into Italian (*molto lento* probably being too fast), but I was learning plenty of the official terminology as I went along in my rather unsynchronised way. Was it healthy to be studying the Grade 4 theory book simultaneously with Grade 6 practical? Purists would doubtless say mastery of the theory should keep pace with the practical, and at best my approach could be described as 'syncopated'. However, the very first piece in the Grade 6 practical syllabus, Couperin's *Les petits moulins à vent,* contained some fine examples of what I referred to as the 'twiddly bits' but which Grade 4 theory insisted were called ornaments. Getting the fingers to play the game was another issue, but at least I should be able to convince some theory examiner that I could recognise a trill when I saw one and knew the difference between a lower and upper mordent, or, for that matter, an acciaccatura and an appoggiatura, and that a turn wasn't just something you did at the end of the page. Once again, applying the theory to real music paid dividends and I began to see light at the end of the tunnel. And even hear the distant drum roll heralding the award of The Certificate. One of the higher grades' challenges was a deepening of knowledge about intervals, not only major, minor and perfect but also augmented and diminished. This was one of those aspects that I sometimes felt I'd conquered and yet at others it completely mystified me. Little diagrams of keyboards, combined with a pencil in each hand, with which I took the given interval, semitone by semitone, back to middle C, the cornerstone of everything, sometimes helped. The secret lay in whether or not both pencils finished up on white keys. Knowing my scales was an even better bet. I practised like mad and at this rate I'd soon be able to distinguish an augmented interval from a diminished one at twelve paces – and that would be four lots of three steps if I were walking in a compound quadruple rhythm. But I still reckoned acciaccatura sounded like something you'd serve with pasta.

A tenuous connection with food leads me to my message, as new Chairman, in the term's e-newsletter. These had only been in circulation since twelve months previously but had proved a useful communication and marketing tool, broadcasting details of our activities and advertising our concerts with no cost and not too much effort. So what's it got to do with food? I'll let the message speak for itself.

Soon after being elected at the recent AGM, I was sent a joke about Chicken Licken, which is unfortunately unrepeatable in polite company. However, it did remind me of another character, the Little Red Hen, whose story I think featured alongside that of Chicken Licken, in the same volume of the Janet and John series on which I cut my literary teeth. It must have been at least Book 4 or 5, as it featured quite complex sentences, with a particular emphasis on the interrogative.

The Little Red Hen was a fussy little madam who tried to get all the other creatures involved in the successive stages leading to the production of a cake. *"Who will help me sow the seeds ... Who will help me grind the corn ... Who will help me milk the cow ... Who will help me churn the butter ... Who will help me bake the cake?"* said she, but each time the response was underwhelming. *"Not I,"* said the pig. *"Not I,"* said the goat. *"Not I,"* said the goose. *"Not I,"* said the dodo. Actually, I made that one up, but nevertheless it was rather a long time ago. Undeterred, she vowed to take care of it all herself *"and my five little chicks will help me."* The moral – there always was one – came when the Little Red Hen asked, *"Who will help me eat the cake?"* The sudden rush of volunteers was dismissed, and the only ones to enjoy that privilege were her loyal and helpful offspring.

Thankfully, although it's daunting to find myself at the sharp end of managing the choir, I don't have to adopt Little Red Hen's hectoring tone, as there are many people who willingly, selflessly, efficiently and intelligently play their part in getting the show on the road – or the cake in the oven. You all know who you are, and I hope you realise how much you're appreciated. Now that we have a policy of fixed terms for officers and committee members, it will become increasingly important for more people to take their turn, so please start thinking now about what skills you could offer in order to give something back to your choir.

Everyone does already fuel the end result, of course, by engaging with the music, learning it week by week and following the MD's lead so our audiences can feast on something tasty.

I hoped this would have the dual effect of thanking and encouraging those who did so much to keep the machinery of the choir moving and also motivating others who didn't, but it needed a suitable parting shot with which to sign off. My predecessor often used to end his emails, especially in challenging situations, with 'onwards and upwards'. I had thought of adapting this to *crescendo ed accelerando*, which as a performance direction literally means 'getting louder and faster', but which I felt could appropriately be loosely paraphrased as 'life's too short to hang back being timid'. This was too pretentious for words, though, of course, so I settled for:

Keep practising!

Two of the key helpers, so to speak, had been the XC (who was still the Chairman at the time) and our digitally dextrous Piano Accompanist (PA), both of whom had been instrumental in the purchase of a new digital piano. This isn't the place to go into detail about why we'd changed rehearsal venue to a different school, but suffice to say the pianos our new home had previously owned had been 'thrown away' for lack of use. Neither is this the place to bemoan what this implies about the status of music in today's curriculum, but it did mean we had to invest in our own.

Research was carried out to ensure we could affordably acquire something of sufficient quality to support a 100-strong choir. A field visit to my local music shop was arranged, and I thought my involvement would be limited to showing the way. It turned out, though, that it would be helpful for the PA to hear someone else play so she could more dispassionately judge the instrument from a distance. Playing in the middle of the High Street made an interesting change from playing in the corner of my kitchen (yes, really), but it was considerably less daunting than playing for an examiner. I didn't stumble too much through a delicate Chopin waltz that I'd been labouring over for about three months ... then the PA took one look at the music and played it beautifully straight off. Oh well. The main thing was, she was smitten with the piano, so we bought it on the spot, having measured up to find that we'd be able to store it on its back in our designated understage cupboard – it was compact but just too tall to go in upright.

The XC then revealed extraordinary carpentry skills that he'd kept hidden under his mantle of academic wisdom. Many's the time his emails would blind me with science, and I usually tackled them with a dictionary at the ready. His evident practical bent meant that the piano could be safely manoeuvred from cupboard to rehearsal position, and vice-versa, aboard a sturdy customised trolley, with a wooden casing then fitted over the whole caboodle, incorporating handles and pulleys to lower it onto its back. All this was achieved efficiently and without danger of damage either to the piano or the physique of the willing rota of removal men and women (mostly men, to be fair).

When the XC sent me a message announcing that he was planning to fit some larger castors, it coincided with one of my not unusual episodes of needing to be in several places at once. Could he perhaps equip me with castors, too?

'No problem. Would you like fixed wheels or castor action; rubber tyres or do you prefer to be heard on approach?'

'Can they be made to play *Arrival of the Queen of Sheba*?'

'The trouble with trying to assemble a music-playing skate is that the frequency must rise as the wheel rotation speed increases. Therefore not only would you

34

tend to become a coloratura soprano but because of the inexact note intervals, consequent on the continuous, rather than quantal, range of velocities, *Arrival of the Queen of Sheba* might be converted to the modal, possibly even the HypoMixolydian (which would be dreadful!) I hope you see my problem. As you can tell I have been looking at my dictionary of music again and the bit about modals is actually quite interesting.'

I blame the MD.

As we were respectively supposed to be getting on with other things, I decided this email exchange had to stop. 'In that case I'll settle for a set of stilts to add stature, not to mention placing me nearer the high notes', I wrote, and altered the subject line to 'Stop it and get on with your work'.

We didn't foresee any queens arriving for our performances, but the CM had been beavering away with her concert-managing deadlines and gleefully announced that we'd need to reserve seats at both occasions for visiting dignitaries. Full marks in the profile-raising stakes, as we were to welcome the Chair of Council to our rural church setting, and the Mayor to our city venue, each accompanied by their consorts. The terminology fascinated me, especially in relation to the female Mayor. Being married to a schoolteacher for a couple of decades, I had grown fairly used to being known as 'sir's wife', and I considered that perhaps it was high time for 'sir' to be restyled 'the Chairman's Consort' (CC).

It also brought a particular poignancy to a phrase from the *Mystical Songs ... Consort both heart and lute* ...sung the first time with a tied crotchet and quaver but the second with just the crotchet, and woe betide anyone who put the 't' on late, or too pronounced. That was also one of the few sections where the sopranos split into two parts, which was an extra dimension for me to contend with as a 'second', since my natural inclination was to consort too closely with the 'firsts' who had the tune. Dissecting the *Mystical Songs* in minute detail and getting a more secure grip on the harmonies was rather different from my original encounter with them. Our ongoing progress coincided with publication of an article I'd written several months earlier for the Royal College of Organists:

> *Let all the world in every corner sing! The corner in question on a sunny Saturday in May was the centre of the second city. Or more precisely, St Philip's Cathedral, a haven from Birmingham's hustle and bustle, where the Royal College of Organists welcomed around 100 strangers from around the country to its Sing Fauré event.*

> *Throughout our afternoon rehearsal, tourists would step inside to admire the richness of Edward Burne-Jones' windows, achieved by a palette of more shades of red stained glass than I thought imaginable. The visitors lingered a while, witnessing a living church, as Peter Wright guided us through the intricacies of Fauré's serene Requiem and Vaughan Williams' Five Mystical Songs. Peter was supported by Stuart Nicholson's fine accompaniment on the organ, its gleaming pipes echoing the gold roses on the ceiling. No pipes 'en chamade', though, but I did learn what this meant when Peter graphically exhorted the tenors (all ten of them) to make one of their entries sound like a fanfare.*

> *It's such juicy morsels that make these 'come and sing' events so worthwhile and memorable. In three hours' rehearsal you can't realistically hope to attain the same performance standard as you would with the customary three months – although our select late-afternoon audience clearly enjoyed it – but an unfamiliar*

conductor's perspective is always valuable. The day could just as easily have been entitled String Fauré, as Peter advocated singing like violins, preparing for the note by having the bow already moving, as it were, and keeping it on the string through the long notes. I have a newfound respect for my vocal cords.

Peter complimented us at this, his last official engagement as President of the RCO, for being one of the most receptive groups he'd ever worked with. He got some blank looks, however, when trying to illustrate some timing tips with reference to the bouncing balls of karaoke. He was on safer territory when he shifted the analogy to the Dambusters, but safest of all, of course, is nothing new – watch the conductor!

No matter how familiar the music – and who could resist Fauré's ethereal Requiem, with a sweetly lyrical Pie Jesu sung on this occasion by soprano Ruth Houghton – there's always something new to appreciate. With the absence of orchestral accompaniment, the dramatic bars of organ solo in the Sanctus brought the piece to a climax with renewed poignancy and reinforced the impact of light and shade. Vaughan Williams certainly presented plenty of challenges. Unlike baritone soloist Chi-Hoe Mak, whose wonderfully clear diction revealed he knew every note and word, for most of the participants it was sight-reading time! Apart from a fulfilling experience in its own right, this for me was useful preparation for my own choir's celebration of Vaughan Williams later in the year, when the Mystical Songs will no longer be such a mystery.

The applause died down and it was time to go. We trailed out of the Cathedral to find the heat of the day had bubbled up into a downpour. This didn't dampen the spirits, though, as everyone headed back, some as far afield as Essex, Cumbria and Buckinghamshire, to their own particular corner of the world.

Encouraged by seeing my work in print, I asked the RCO if they might give me a discount for their next event if I provided another write-up afterwards.

'You can come at RCO member rate – how's that?'

I wasn't totally bowled over by the £3 off that this represented, but on reflection considered that being an Hon MRCO, even if only for a day, would definitely be worth writing about. Especially as I didn't have a clue how to drive an organ.

Back to a slightly different corner of the world, not a million miles away geographically or even in style, but quite a departure in age range, I took some time out to investigate the university music department. My discussions with Kevin were of necessity couched in the conditional tense, as not only did I have to see how our other collaborative efforts developed, but also the MD wouldn't be able to commit to anything until he'd seen and heard the students in action. Easier said than done. No matter, as it gave me a good excuse to gatecrash their choir practice. As anticipated, there was a great buzz to be had from singing with a crowd of bright young things, with their lives ahead of them for the development of their undoubted talents. One 20-year-old was even given the dubious honour of conducting her own 'Happy Birthday to You', which made rather a change from our recent rendition to our two most senior members with their combined age of 176!

The hour's rehearsal flew by, with a warm up emphasising the importance of good breathing, followed by Christmas music taken from a variety of books which were passed around with astounding energy. The most salutary part, though, was when each section learned just a few wordless bars without any reference to the printed page at all, conquering their own melody and rhythm before attempting to put it all together. After a reasonable bash at it, we were finally allowed to see it in its context, which turned out to be a setting of *Away in a Manger*. Kevin's verdict after we sang from the score: 'you did it better without!'

As befits an educational establishment, the students weren't just told what to sing but opinions were sought as to their informed choices. One of the lads at the back let the music do the talking, by breaking out into an unmistakably African number, apparently not just his favourite from the previous Christmas repertoire but a popular choice all round as everyone else irrepressibly joined in. You could virtually hear the drumbeats. Perhaps that would find its way into the carol service again, which was going to have to be a good one because it would be the Chaplain's 43rd and last before retirement. A reminder of the power of singing to break down age barriers.

November
A choir by any other name

Once I'd made the portentous joint concert announcement, I felt that more than enough energy had been expended in getting us that far. 'Let there be a *Creation*-free zone for a couple of weeks,' I declared, and this was met with a collective sigh of relief. Vaughan Williams needed a bit of TLC – and so did one rather bemused Chairman. Everyone had earned their half-term break, then it was back to it, to add some finesse to the *Mystical Songs* and *Fantasia*, and also to learn a whole raft of songs that hadn't even been touched on. In only five rollicking weeks!

Rollicking was certainly the epithet to apply to Vaughan Williams' arrangement of the *Wassail Song*, for which the technical term was a new one on me: 'through-composed'. I learned that this meant that, instead of each verse being essentially the same music, this freely arranged version was a more continuous linear whole, with variations between verses, and the melody effectively passed from voice to voice. Rather like the sharing of the wassail bowl (from *wes hal*, old English for 'Be thou hale/whole', a festive drinking salutation). Complex, challenging, but a lot of fun, and if practised right at the end of rehearsal, impossible to shake out of your head!

I made another discovery on the back of this new knowledge. One of the basses lacking a *Wassail* score asked for advice on whether he'd found the right one. 'No,' I said, and went on to show off my understanding of through-composed. 'What you have there is the one where everyone sings in unison.' Oh no they don't. They sing everything at the same time, yes, which for half a century had been my take on 'unison', but if I'd applied the linguistic side of my brain to it, it would have been resoundingly obvious it also had to do with tone. Dictionary of musical terms for Christmas, please. And one wassail bowl, size XXL.

The choir's sense of timing and partnership was set a rather different challenge when an assorted crowd of members, family and friends turned out for a one-off social evening which exercised the legs more than the vocal cords. Strictly Barn Dancing. As a means of losing one's inhibitions, this is definitely to be recommended, although it has to be said my *dos-y-dos* was a little more sluggish after the fish and chip supper, and should a choir with an Equal Opportunities policy really be dancing the Gay Gordons? It occurred to me that this would be an excellent way of cementing the *entente cordiale* when we welcomed our French visitors again, but we'd need a bilingual Caller and some of the terminology made music theory sound positively straightforward. One dance, for example, was styled upon the rutting of deer, with the technical term 'rant' applied to a splendid foot shuffle that occurred at regular intervals. The XC's ranting was a thing to behold, incidentally. And how on earth would you translate Strip the Willow? Losing inhibitions is one thing, but it could be in danger of being taken too far.

The question was, could we even understand each other in our own language? When I received a phone call from The Other Choir's chairman, which started with the words 'we're not having this conversation, but …', I felt I'd strayed into a James Bond script. This cloak and dagger stuff didn't seem like my style, so I roped in the GB to share the top secret knowledge. The Other Choir's AGM was to feature a motion to pursue discussions with us about permanent amalgamation, which my counterpart expected would be welcomed by his members. 'It's all happening rather quickly,' he said. Oh no, it's not, I thought, not unless we say so.

There followed a bombardment of email exchanges between me and the team, underlining that we must make sure we remained in control of events. I was particularly insistent that we didn't backtrack on our original intention to evaluate joint rehearsals and Creation concert before considering anything longer term.

Email communication in itself has a tendency to speed everything up, of course, and I'm sure that horrible management-speak phrase for keeping everyone well informed – 'up to speed' – is no coincidence. At my more nostalgic, I'd find myself longing for the days of snail-mail, phone calls and face to face encounters with real live human beings. The added danger of emails circulating around a group of people is that some hit 'reply all' whereas some just hit 'reply', and it's easy to get confused over who's been told what. I noticed that a significant message didn't seem to have been sent to the VC, so I forwarded a copy, only for him to say he'd had it anyway. 'Perhaps I'm a BCC,' he suggested. For the uninitiated, this stands for Blind Carbon Copy, whereby the sender can forward you the message without the other recipients seeing your email address – whether from a data protection point of view or whatever other reasons of secrecy. On the other hand, I couldn't resist my own alternative translation: 'Beloved Choral Colleague'.

The VC/BCC was in danger of landing himself with far too many epithets, in fact. I noticed a subsidiary title of Publicity Manager had already crept in, as though being my Vice were not sufficient. A GP in real life, he's also a talented linguist, so it seemed natural enough to refer my other colleagues to him, as 'my favourite polyglot', should they need any grammatical advice when keeping all GB deliberations in the conditional. That particular missive was signed off with 'Keep humouring me' (Imperative).

Thereafter my correspondence with the VC became an email Babylon, umpteen languages dredged up from pre-choir days. I was reminded of my first French teacher, Mr Hershon, incongruously a Jew in a girls' Church of England school, who not only fired my fascination for foreign languages but also taught us a wonderful Yiddish song with those unmistakable lilting rhythms. Then there was the formidable Mrs Briggs, an archetypal battleaxe who virtually dragged us through Latin O Level. Although a torment at the time, I realised even then the value of this apparently dead language as a strong foundation for other linguistic endeavours. But what I failed to appreciate was how it was going to come in handy once I took up choral singing. I suppose you can sing a Requiem without knowing the ins and outs of declensions and conjugations, but it enriches the experience knowing roughly what's going on with the language as well as the music. My trip down the scholastic memory lane wouldn't be complete in the context of words and music without a mention of the school chaplain, who would always greet the assembled throng with the words 'Good morning girlsssssss', to which we would dutifully reply 'Good morning Father Batessssss' like a load of hissing vipers. I have since mastered the almost imperceptible terminal 's', of course.

It was around now that I decided to address my state of ignorance as far as *The Creation* was concerned, and bought myself a recording. Time to see what all the fuss was about. Vaughan Williams was ousted temporarily from the car's CD player and I drove my way through one and a half discs without thinking much about it. Maybe I was concentrating on the road. Then I suddenly noticed a rather lively, involved number. 'Gosh, this is good,' I mused, only then to ponder 'wait a minute, why's it in Latin?' Our version was to be in English, as opposed to the alternative German – in fact, I'd already privately remarked that we seemed to be having an English-only year, which was slightly unusual and mildly frustrating, and which would have me seeking out foreign stuff elsewhere as the year wore on. All was revealed when I realised I'd been completely oblivious to *Creation's* raucous finale, and had strayed into a completely different work of Haydn's, *Insanae et Vanae Curae.* Better pay more attention in rehearsals.

The Other Choir's AGM confirmed that, sure enough, they wanted to press on with negotiations on a merger. Nestling within another email exchange was a throw-away comment that whatever else needed deciding, at least a new name had already been agreed. Heckles rising, I challenged our GB members, who reassured me that nothing of the sort had been agreed. Just as well. The surest way of sparking controversy is to discuss ladies' concert dress. The next sure way is to float the idea of a name-change. In fact, I'd long thought, along with others, that our name was far too long-winded and geographically inaccurate, to boot. To use an outrageously exaggerated antipodean analogy, it would be a bit like calling ourselves the Alice Springs and District Choral Society and performing at the Sydney Opera House. Mind you, how about that for a suitably large venue for *Creation?* Suffice to say, agreeing any new name would require nerves of steel and at this stage was way down the list of priorities, although it seemed most likely that the City's name would have to feature if the local authority's grants were up for grabs. For now, the hypothetical new entity would be known as 'New Choir'. With the emphasis on the hypothetical. If only we could have the emphasis on the 'Choir' and get on with the music.

Just when we thought The Other Choir had run out of surprises for us, it transpired that their MD, who was thought to have been about to vacate his position after their Christmas concerts, would take their *Creation* rehearsals after all for the first half of term, rather than his assistant. Not that this needed to imply any warning bells, but it was another example of moving goalposts and I couldn't help wondering whether I'd need to invest in a red card.

Meanwhile, I certainly seemed to be getting the hang of commanding our own choir's attention. When I broke the news about the latest developments, there was scarcely a murmur. Had they all fallen asleep, I wondered? But no, a smattering of emails commenting on the news revealed that they were interested rather than apathetic, and that I'd hit the right balance in how much information was being imparted. The more I answered members individually, emphasising that each person's view counted, the more it struck home that my own personal opinion – whatever that might be – would need to remain subsidiary to my main role of keeping the peace. Now we'd come this far, whatever the outcome, some would like it and some wouldn't. Crash course in diplomacy, here we come.

And now for something rather different. When a single soprano gatecrashed a men-only singing workshop, there were two ways of looking at it. One, it was incredibly satisfying to be serenaded by 80 male voices, some a little apprehensive but the majority eager and enthusiastic. And two, it was frustrating not to be able to join in. But it was my notebook I'd warmed up, not my vocal cords, for this 'No Girls Allowed' session, part of a project to get more men singing.

Talking of warm-ups, once City of Birmingham Symphony Chorus (CBSC) Director Simon Halsey had remarked how wonderful it was to be surrounded by so many hairy males for a change, he spent a full 15 minutes getting them to limber up. Literally. It was the most physical warm-up I'd ever witnessed, with lots of stretching – men's joints being far noisier than women's, incidentally – punching, kicking, and of course singing – scales, arpeggios and just single sustained sounds, rattling around the full height of the CBSO Centre's pale wooden rafters.

Simon, casual in grey jumper and jeans, and assisted by Julian Wilkins at the piano, skilfully encouraged awareness of different kinds of sound and how to produce them, whether nasal or brighter, vowels or consonants.

From the first bone-crunching stretch, the men were hooked. Over delicious pre-workshop nibbles, I'd asked one group of friendly-looking chaps why they'd decided to come. In unison, each pointed at one particular colleague and declared 'he made me!' Some visitors were used to singing in other choirs, some hadn't ever tried it before, some were rusty, some had been tempted by an advert on the radio or in a concert programme. None of them looked disappointed by what they found.

An ambitious booklet of music had been prepared, kicking off with a unison version of Ralph Vaughan Williams' folk song *Linden Lea.* Two things immediately struck me: concentration was absolute, and it was a stunning sound. Simon confirmed this by congratulating the men for being, somewhat to his surprise, 'completely in tune' and 'beautifully blended'. Nevertheless, he urged more from them by means of techniques to create and project the purest quality of sound and the most expressive dynamics. 'Your diction's excellent,' he said, 'now tell me a story.'

It was just a month until Christmas, so there was a festive feel to the next couple of pieces. *Three Kings from Persian Lands Afar* was again sung in unison, a sensuous and lyrical line that was less familiar to me than Julian's piano accompaniment, which captured my own choir's harmonies in preparation for an item in our imminent concerts, when the tune would be sung by a baritone soloist. Simon took the men through the melody phrase by phrase, encouraging them to convey through their singing an exotic, desirable, spice-laden atmosphere. 'Colour it like a Shakespearean actor.'

Then the fun really started, with some part-singing! Simon prefaced the first run-through of *God rest you merry gentlemen* with the comment that he'd rarely seen such a large group of tenors. Alluding to the fabulous tours the CBSC occasionally undertakes, he underlined the value placed on tenors by claiming that they're never all allowed to travel on the same plane!

After this dose of praise, the tenors lost it a bit once they stopped being in charge of 'the tune'. As a second soprano, I could completely identify with this, and willed them to get it right once they'd been drilled through a sectional rehearsal. The resulting success proved that if a group's big enough, everyone has the courage to have a go. It was clear that singing in harmony also presented added challenges in timing and rhythm, and I'm sure that an extra rendition would have given greater security in keeping up with each other – but it was time for a foray into the world of light opera.

The repartee between Simon and Julian was quite theatrical in itself. Turning to a whole page of wordless music at the start of a Gilbert and Sullivan march, Simon said, 'Julian will now give a performance.' Looking askance, Julian replied, 'Play the piano, you mean?'

Several virtuoso minutes later, I'm sure everyone agreed with Simon, then had a great deal of fun with lyrics and music alike.

For a different perspective on choral singing, Simon brought the men down from their raked seating to stand in a grand circle around him 'like a huge Stonehenge.' This enabled them to interact visually and also hear each other better – and for a bystander like me it was magical too. As they resumed their seats, beaming, I heard many exclamations of 'that was amazing!'

Last in the book – they achieved all five pieces in a mere hour and a half, and with some distinction – was *Linden Lea* yet again, but in four parts this time. This helped to consolidate what they'd been learning throughout the evening, although I suspected the lasting impression would be of fun rather than education.

The men's workshop idea was set to be developed further, as Simon hoped the CBSC would be the first European choir to boast 50 of each voice type. I was sure some of the participants would be keen to audition. But in the unlikely event they didn't want to join Simon's gang, they'd be very welcome in mine.

As my gang was edging towards those all-important concert dates, it was time to tackle some of the practical issues. Tickets and posters were printed and distributed, a start was made on the concert programme, and something tempting was concocted to send to the press. It was also time to forewarn everyone to turn up in the right gear, the announcement of which required a deep breath. Ladies' concert dress was a subject guaranteed to provoke heated debate, although it shouldn't, as we did have an agreed system: long black skirts or formal trousers, with white tops at Christmas, black tops at Easter, and something more colourful in the summer. The men were always trouble-free, scrubbing up well and sporting non-controversial DJs. The previous Easter, before it really had anything to do with me, although I'd just agreed to stand for Chairman, I found myself in the wrong place at the wrong time and the then Chairman raised his eyebrows at me for advice on how to answer the question 'what sleeve length?' Not exactly in the mood, my off-the-cuff response was 'I really don't think it matters', but this clearly wasn't considered good enough and the murmurs continued. Irritating though it was, the best approach was always to look for the funny side. The following day being April Fools' Day, I sent an email, headed 'Any colour as long as it's black', to the Chair, the MD and my soon-to-be VC:

'Chairman-elect-dom has gone to my head and I've made an executive decision that ladies' concert dress shall comprise sleeves that go down to their ankles.* Due to the practical page-turning impediment thus created, it has also been decided to perform without scores. Should these new regulations prove successful, they will be extended to instrumental performers and the conductor. Please let me know if you foresee any insurmountable problems. If, for example, it was felt there would simply be too much fabric on stage and not enough flesh on view, I would consider redressing the balance by making the men wear shorts.
* For concerts on 1st April only. Less absurd comments may follow if I have the strength.'

The future VC expressed grave reservations about airing his legs in public, whereas the MD's suggestion wasn't about clothing at all:

'Could we go for coordinated hairdos - it would look so much smarter if all ladies were peroxided and 'bouffanté' - perhaps all men could be instructed to part their hair on the left.'

That was all very well, but I'd long before made a conscious decision to grow grey gracefully, so this was my counter-response: '... the MD ought to stand out from the crowd, of course, so I'll bleach my hair the day you get your barber to give you a Gustavo Dudamel...' Our MD shared much of the exuberance and enthusiasm of the young Venezuelan conductor, but not his wild black locks.

Back to November, and I found the perfect opportunity to raise the subject after one of our valiant efforts to conquer Vaughan Williams' fiendish Wassail Song. One of the characters in the story of general revelry is the 'maid in the lily white smock', so I blithely said 'so that solves our problems about concert dress this time, eh, ladies?' To be on the safe side, I also suggested that, as long as nobody opted for basques or spaghetti straps, any sleeve length for the white tops would do just fine. I should have known better than to mention it at all, as one of the new members collared me at home-time, advocating something bright and beautiful as more appropriate for Christmas time. Presumably as long as we realise we can't please everyone all the time, we'll never be disappointed.

At least I didn't have to put up with the treatment dished out to St Cecilia. By chance I happened upon a radio commemoration of the patron saint of music and musicians, her saint's day falling on 22nd November. Coinciding with lunchtime wasn't the greatest timing, though, as the description of her martyrdom was rather grizzly. Suffice to say she didn't give up easily and went down fighting. And singing.

December
A Vaughan-Williams smorgasbord

December was always destined to be an all and nothing sort of month. So much was crammed into the first couple of weeks, even leaving aside any personal Christmas preparations. The previous year the choir had taken the unusual step of performing two Christmas concerts, in different venues on consecutive weeks, and this had proved so successful that we seemed to have set ourselves a precedent. Besides, after all the work that goes into preparing for one concert, why not have double the fun of performing it all over again? Or double the trouble, depending which way you looked at it.

Then, after all the intensity, a long lull, filled with choral withdrawal symptoms before the new year and new term. But that comes later.

A few days before December was ushered in, the CM, in risk assessment mode, had circulated some contingency plans in case any of the main players – MD, soloist, organist, instrumentalists – were defeated by traffic or bad weather and couldn't make it on the day. The thought appalled me. It seemed like she had second sight, though, as our final Monday rehearsal, 1st December, was almost scuppered.

I returned from my morning piano lesson – without any grand progress having been demonstrated, it has to be said – to find missed calls from the MD on both my landline and mobile. This was unusual in the extreme, and I sensed a calamity. Two minutes, a couple of texts and a phone call later, I found out he'd landed in some East Anglian ditch after a head-on collision on icy roads. He claimed he was unhurt, but sounded a little the worse for wear and clearly there was a large question mark hanging over that evening's rehearsal.

Masquerading as someone who knew how to handle a crisis, I instructed him not to worry about anything to do with the choir and just get himself sorted out, keeping me posted of developments. I'd do the worrying about the choir – in fact it gave me something to take my mind off my next appointment, going under the dentist's drill.

What was the best plan of campaign if the MD couldn't make it? At any other stage in the term, we could have got away with cancelling the rehearsal, but this seemed totally unthinkable five days before our first concert. We didn't have an obvious substitute, but I hoped that at a push we could have a general run-through with our accompanist at the helm. The PA agreed that to cancel didn't bear thinking about and she volunteered to do her best single-handed – well, two hands on the piano, but just the one and only loyal PA. I fired off another reassuring text to the MD, who replied that he'd make it after all, chauffeured (an hour and a half in each direction) by his wife. Living proof that beside every great man there's a wonderful woman.

As everyone was assembling, I hopped up on the podium to let them know what had happened, so the MD didn't have to relive the accident himself. 'Make sure you're all on your best behaviour, please, as he mustn't have any more stress!' Thus it was that, by the time the MD arrived in his whiplashed state, the choir were practising Vaughan Williams' *Old Hundredth*, under the PA's direction, as though their lives depended on it.

Fragile though the MD was – and it was the only time I've ever seen him sitting down to conduct – by the end of the rehearsal he'd visibly loosened up. I put this down to three things: his own cheerful determination, the choir's strengthened sense of teamwork, and the healing power of the music itself.

No matter that some people said they enjoyed belonging to the choir simply for Monday evening rehearsals, performances were a fact of life. I was conscious that the success or otherwise of our first Vaughan Williams concert would be the first real test of how I was measuring up as Chairman. Or, to put it more accurately, how effectively I was employing those crucial delegation skills. Would the programme be ready for printing on time? Would everyone turn up in the right outfits? Would we ever find a page-turner for the organist? Had I been sufficiently persuasive about ticket sales and would we get an audience larger than the choir itself? On all counts, just about. There were a few extraneous cardigans, shawls and scarves over the lily white smocks, and although it was a bitterly cold day, this didn't go without comment from the CM.

Her contingency plans thankfully weren't required, though and, barring one or two choir members who sadly didn't make it due to illness, we had all the right people in the right place at the right time. The right place was a beautiful old church in a picturesque rural village setting. The right time was 2.00pm, as we would always have an afternoon rehearsal on the big day, to warm us up, get used to the acoustics and put everything together with musicians and soloists.

Just beforehand there'd been a wedding, so the church was adorned with a fragrant archway of crimson and ivory flowers, echoed by decorations on the pew-ends. These presented a slight technical hitch when it came to processing to our seats. The appointment of a Stage Manager had been a relatively recent and hugely successful innovation. Instead of the choir assuming their places in dribs and drabs, the SM marshalled us into a well-disciplined cohort of choristers with a definite plan of how to grace the stage and then leave it again, even down to scores uniformly tucked under left arms.

At this particular venue, the configuration of the church meant our only option was to file down the centre aisle and take to our places alternating those on the left with those on the right – or 'unzipping', to use the SM's technical term – and reversing the process on the way out (zipping, presumably). Add the MD's podium and music stand into the equation, and the already narrow nave became something of an obstacle course. So it was that spectators in the first couple of rows would find the floral displays popped over the top of the pew momentarily while the choir traipsed in.

The right people included baritone soloist, Håkan Vramsmo, a charming young Swede with a rich, resonant voice. In Church House, the annexe that we could use between rehearsal and performance, he knocked back lemon and honey, having only just recovered from losing his voice altogether. It occurred to me that Christmas concerts could helpfully be scheduled in the more healthy summer months. Told you I liked to do things differently.

After weeks of rehearsing the various works in bits and pieces and according to what required the most attention, it was always gratifying to put it all together in a logical order. In this instance, some inspired programming meant we fulfilled the double brief of celebrating the life of Ralph Vaughan Williams as well as getting everyone in the mood for Christmas. The first half, punctuated by interesting and illuminating snippets of information from the MD, included hymns and anthems, some for choir alone, some inviting audience participation, and a couple of preludes for organ solo. Vaughan Williams' *Rhosymedre* prelude, heralding the singing of *Author of Life Divine*, was an unknown gem to me and proved an unexpected treat. The hymn itself wasn't that well-known, to be frank, since it had only found its way into rehearsals a couple of weeks before, but I think we made a convincing job of it. Leading into the interval, the choir supported Håkan's interpretation of the *Five Mystical Songs,* culminating in the inspiring Antiphon *Let all the world in every corner sing.* The final notes fanfared forth from a hundred mouths, and hung in the hallowed space for just long enough to savour the triumph before appreciative applause.

The second half was the Christmassy bit. The audience entered enthusiastically into the spirit of some familiar carols and looked suitably moved by those delivered by the choir, again with an emphasis on Vaughan Williams' music. All the preparation for the *Fantasia on Christmas Carols* paid off, even down to those shifting time signatures. A kind of compendium of traditional English carols, it was Christmas in a nutshell. Then it was time for Christmas in a wassail bowl, and thankfully this more or less worked too, or at least all the revellers finished up together even if they staggered around a little along the way. As if that wasn't enough festive spirit, we topped it all off with an encore, *We wish you a merry Christmas.* Try singing that, in a fabulous arrangement, surrounded by a like-minded team, after a couple of hours – no, a whole term – of hard work, and I'd suggest it's impossible to finish off without a beaming smile. We'd certainly earned our figgy pudding.

The following morning when I discovered a missed call from the MD from 10 o'clock the night before, when I would have been driving home, I jumped to the rather irrational conclusion of yet another car accident. A last-ditch and belated text to check why he'd called revealed merely that he was fine and judged the concert a success. Light dawned a bit later when the CM confessed that she'd inadvertently locked him and Håkan in Church House, when they were getting changed after the concert. Thankfully the Church Warden went to check and they made their escape. Carefully avoiding any wisecracks such as 'I've heard of a captive audience, but this is ridiculous', I accepted full responsibility and promised to leave the phone on at key moments and keep all contact numbers at the ready.

During our Monday rehearsal, when there was a definite, repetitive emphasis on ironing out a few glitches in the Wassail Song, I couldn't help but notice how frequently that wretched maid in the lily white smock 'trip'd to the door and pull'd back the lock to let those jolly wassailers walk in'. She could have made herself useful on Saturday night. This rehearsal took place in what would allegedly be 'concert formation', albeit without the infamous raked staging that we use at the city church. But first the SM and I had to establish that we could use our usual practice hall. This wasn't very convenient for the caretaking staff, who had to shift exam desks, but our dubious faces, on a site visit that morning to check out an alternative room, convinced them that we needed to stay put. The SM gallantly went back in the afternoon to assist with furniture removal. By the evening he'd worn grooves in the road.

After the initial to-ing and fro-ing to get everyone settled into their correct places, the rehearsal got underway and seemed very successful, promising an even better second concert. A sense of elation was shattered when one of my soprano colleagues pointed out that three of the 'poor first sopranos' had been out on a limb alongside the seconds, rather than in the firsts' block. This less than helpful timing, right at the end when it was too late to do anything about it, elicited an equally less than professional response. An apologetic phone call on my part therefore ensued the following day, and everything was smoothed over. We'd have a bit of a re-shuffle on Saturday.

Meanwhile, midweek saw me enjoying somebody else's choral efforts, at the University carol service. There was plenty to join in with, but without the pressure of giving a performance. Students and staff alike took this as a cue to start to relax after a busy term and get into the festive spirit, helped in no small measure by mulled wine and mince pies served afterwards. The service had a particular poignancy for me after rehearsing with the University Choir, and it was heartening to hear how much progress they'd made with their party pieces in those couple of months. *What child is this?* with the Greensleeves arrangement, went especially well, as did Stan's own composition *Kings came riding,* with its lively swing rhythm. There were one or two surprises. The setting of *Away in a Manger,* with the unfamiliar section first learned by rote rather than from the scores, formed a hushed backdrop to the University prayer, unusually read in Welsh. And – perhaps not such a surprise – the service concluded with *Jabula Jesu,* the Zulu folk song so spontaneously extemporised at the rehearsal back in October.

Being a university with a thriving deaf community and great strength in Deaf Studies, carol services were always signed throughout – carols, reading, prayers, the lot. The high point for me was a 'reading' about the shepherds, signed in total silence by our hugely respected deaf lecturer, wearing his recently-awarded MBE. Those unfamiliar with sign language could read the text in the programme if they wished, but John told the story with such passion that I preferred to watch and marvel. Watching the signers interpreting the carols, and recognising some of the 'translations' – 'the running of the deer' from *The holly and the ivy* was particularly gorgeous – doubled the significance of the words somehow. It occurred to me how important it is, for a choir presenting words and music alone, without the matching visual images, to bring those words to life with immaculate diction.

Armed with that thought, I was impatient to get stuck into Saturday's concert. Everyone arranged themselves to their satisfaction at the afternoon rehearsal, accompanied this time by a string orchestra as well as organ, and with Håkan making a welcome return. In the evening the mayor and her consort turned up as arranged, as did the Chairman's Consort and children. As well as my number one fan, my Mum. The very respectable audience wasn't quite a sell-out, but there were more than enough to gladden the heart of the Treasurer. Not to mention how satisfying it is to sing to an almost-full house. Not surprisingly, the fun and games came in the interval, with something of a scrum to get served with drinks. Thinking ahead to our Easter concert, with a double choir and, if all went to plan, even larger audience, the best bet might be to issue interval drinks on arrival.

Whatever the practical niceties, the fact was that the concert was a stunner. Even if I still didn't quite get those entries right in the Wassail Song.

How would we follow that? Well, there was a social evening scheduled for the Monday, ostensibly a chance to let our hair down and relax. However, the HS had us taxing our intellectual capabilities as she'd organised a music quiz. She had her own little team of markers, and the word 'scores' took on a whole fresh meaning. Some members had arranged themselves into sextets already. My daughter, who came along more as honorary photographer than to show off her classical music knowledge, joined me, the XC and soprano Eileen, who looked suitably brainy. No sooner had we chosen our team name – Musical Chairs – than the MD arrived looking teamless, so we quickly commandeered him for one our spare seats. Surely we now stood a chance, even though we were still down on numbers? Sadly, we were only runners-up to those swots, The Robins. Perhaps we could have done better if we'd taken it a bit more seriously. The proud holder of a Blue Peter badge, I should have known that the programme's theme tune was called *Barnacle Bill*. I still maintain that we should have been awarded extra points for my perfect pronunciation of *Concierto de Aranjuez*, although I did rather spoil the effect by attributing this guitar classic to Granados rather than Rodrigo.

Even on this occasion, when I was supposed to be well and truly off-duty, we needed a little conflab of the inner circle. The Other Choir were pushing us for details of next year's likely programme, to include in their annual grant application to the local authority. Not that it would necessarily end up having anything to do with us, of course.

Any deficiencies in my musical prowess that evening I put fairly and squarely down to the fact that I was brewing up a dose of flu. So much for getting into Christmas-preparation mode once the choir festivities were over; several frustrating days spent in bed meant I could forget about piano practice and theory exercises, though I did from time to time risk half an ear on Classic FM's carol offerings.

But Christmas nevertheless got prepared, the happy-family time was fairly trouble-free, and presents seemed to have been chosen wisely. So while everyone else's noses were buried in the pages of Michael Parkinson's autobiography or *1001 Ridiculous Ways to Die*, I dipped in and out of musical definitions galore. Time, for example, to understand the hemiola once and for all. Not some strange disease of the blood, but something that kept cropping up in choral sessions, causing havoc with the timing of certain passages, two notes being sung in the time of three or vice-versa and often straddling bar lines. Even if it still held a degree of mystery, at least I could now add gravitas to my pseudo-understanding by referring to it as a 'rhythmic device'.

Since there would be no choir practice until the new year, this music-less hiatus should have given me a nudge in the direction of the piano. I did indulge in the odd half-hour, happy to find that my recently flu-gripped fingers hadn't totally forgotten where to go. If only they displayed the same fluency as they did on the computer keyboard, I'd be bashing out the demisemiquavers like nobody's business. The plaintive stateliness of Kalinnikov's *Chanson Triste* was sufficiently slow for me to be in with a chance. Challenging but reachable – just about, with lots of octave stretches – and oh, what gorgeous chord progressions, that put the sadness into the song. The note in my book indicated I'd first tackled this in early December, so I was quite impressed with myself for mastering a whole piece so quickly that was allegedly around Grade 6 standard. On second thoughts, perhaps 'mastering' is an exaggeration, but I enjoyed playing it anyway.

The thought of a Grade 6 exam wasn't exercising any magnetism for me, and yet I was still determined to make myself eligible for it by passing Grade 5 theory. And this is what grabbed most of my attention as one year slipped into the next. *Accelerando* personified, I stormed my way through a sheaf of Grade 4 practice papers. It might turn out to be a case of 'more haste, less speed', of course, but you can't beat a bit of enthusiasm (well you can, but it has to be at a fast tempo) and the more complex it became, the more fascinating I found it. Yes, I had reached that weird state where I wished to learn music theory for its own sake! Was this normal, or even healthy? While the rest of the world were queuing up for NEXT bargains and Debenhams Blue Cross give-aways, I made a civilised trip to the music shop for my Grade 5 workbook. It was blue and shiny, with impressive-sounding topics in the contents list, like 'transposition', 'composing a melody' and 'chords at cadential points'.

Although risking falling into bad habits, I wanted to press on with it rather than wait for piano lessons to resume, so I decided a bit of DIY-teaching wouldn't do any harm, with ET's reference books at the ready, of course. With a bit of care and attention, there didn't seem to be any pitfalls in the first few sections, so I ploughed my way through exercises in irregular time signatures, the tenor clef, and major and minor keys up to six sharps and flats. I'd already got to grips with playing those scales anyway for the practical, but now it was a case of being precise about how key signatures were written (in four different clefs), spotting where any extra accidentals were needed, and more besides. Musical staves appeared even when my eyes were closed; was this becoming the equivalent of dreaming in a foreign language?

I did take the occasional foray back into real life, of course, thanks to my family. Busily transposing at the kitchen table late one morning, I was accosted by offspring number one: 'What time's lunch?' Closely followed by number two: 'What's for lunch?' Even more closely followed by the CC, who set about building the lunch around me. 'I bet Beethoven never had to put up with this', I grumbled irrelevantly, fretting that Delius' *Walk to the Paradise Garden*, transposed up a 5th from C major and B major to G major and F# major respectively (so that it would sound at concert pitch for horns in F, if you must know) was turning into rather a sprint. 'Pardon?' was the perhaps inevitable response.

January
Delegate with dignity

Before 2009 had got well underway, I would begin to wonder if my year of living musically was turning into a year of existing organisationally, with music in a decidedly secondary role.

But for starters there was the New Year's Day concert from Vienna to soak up, along with a large glass of sherry. All the more exciting since visiting the Musikverein a couple of years earlier, resulting in the following piece for my travel-writing course:

Apart from seeing in the new millennium, I've never been keen on New Year's Eve parties. This is an advantage for a classical music fan like me as it means I get to watch the New Year's Day concert, televised live around the world from Vienna's Musikverein, with a clear head. Waltzes, polkas, and above all the Radetzky March – percussion galore and audience-participatory clapping – would be the worst possible antidote to a hangover. Although tickets for the prime occasion in the golden hall are like gold dust, involving 10-year waiting lists and lotteries, the idea of attending one of the Vienna Philharmonic's other concerts exercised an irresistible magnetism. Narrowly missing Mozart's 250th anniversary, I finally made it for my first visit to the city – and the Musikverein – to celebrate my own half-century.

Even without the greenhousefuls of foliage and floral arrangements that bedeck the stage, organ and balconies for the Neujahrskonzert, the sumptuous over-the-top baroque splendour of the hall immediately assaults the senses. Not for minimalists the rich gilded curlicues surrounding the vibrant blue panels on the ceiling, on which floated paintings of classical maidens, lit by chandeliers cascading with monstrous delicacy, nor the glowing golden caryatids, like elaborate Oscars on steroids, lining the perimeter of the ground floor and balancing the balcony on their heads.

Relinquishing the tourist garb in favour of a posh frock had been a sensible choice, as discord with the elegance and sophistication of expensively perfumed Viennese Society would have been a shame. The music itself delivered harmony of the highest standard. The orchestra interpreted the varying shades of Bruckner's 7th Symphony with balance and passion, building to a climax which filled the Hall with sustained sound and sent shivers up and down the spine like a virtuoso violinist's fingers. A visit to the Vienna Philharmonic's museum revealed that at one point Bruckner had forbidden the Orchestra's playing his 7th, due to bad reviews, but thankfully this sanction had been lifted. Judging by the standing ovation, there were no disappointed customers this time.

The guidebooks argue that no visit to the Austrian capital is complete without experiencing the Opera House, the Staatsoper. Our trip, however, coincided with the annual Opera Ball, so all guided tours were suspended while an army of event organisers erected marquees and traipsed in with crate upon crate of flowers, driven in from Salzburg. The building – once criticised for resembling a railway station – was cocooned by a posse of outside broadcast vehicles.

There was a welcome, however, at Café Aida, diagonally opposite, across the busy interchange where the wide thoroughfare of 'The Ring' allows space for cars, trams, cyclists and pedestrians alike, together with the underground below. Café culture is clearly a part of Viennese everyday life, as we took our coffee – with the traditional glass of water served on the side – rubbing shoulders with shoppers and office-workers rather than tourists. Considering the amount of chocolate and cream consumed, how do the locals keep so slim? In the interests of research one had to sample the sachertorte, a rich cake invented by the Hotel Sacher. Moist chocolate cake is topped with a layer of apricot jam and encased in a generous covering of silky dark chocolate. It was as smooth as the Moonlight Sonata.

On my next visit to Vienna – well, I've still got to see the Opera, after all – I might be tempted to another slice.

The New Year's Day concert on this occasion inevitably featured music by Haydn, who would prove to get everywhere in this, his 200th anniversary year. Composed as an unsubtle hint to his boss, Esterhazy, that the orchestra were missing their families and wanted to go home from the Prince's summer residence where the climate was unpleasant, the *Farewell Symphony* gradually 'lost' musician after musician until eventually the conductor was left on stage all by himself. It occurred to me that if our combined choir turned out to be a bit of a handful for our own forthcoming Haydn work, we could employ such a ruse. Or maybe it would just be the Chairman bidding farewell.

The term started well, though, with a welcome return to getting the lips, lungs and larynx working again. A valiant initial run through *The Creation* revealed that we were in for a terrific sing but also that we'd have our work cut out to do justice to the uplifting choruses and challenging fugues. As always, the first rehearsals had to be devoted to 'notebashing', a necessary preamble to adding style. A bit like knowing how to string letters and words into sentences before enhancing them with imagery. Everyone was encouraged to use a specially-prepared practice disc, with their own voice part highlighted. The soprano line of these aids used to be rendered by the flute, but lately a technique's been perfected to synthesise a human voice – rather tinny and lifeless, but at least you can simultaneously try and learn words and music. It's always a welcome relief, though, once I've grappled with that sufficiently to be able to graduate to an authentic recording and hear everything – all voices plus instruments – in context. It never ceases to amaze me that for some members, our performance is the first time they hear a work in its entirety. For me to be anywhere near confident enough, I have to virtually force-feed my ears.

For a large chunk of the first half of term we had sectional men's and women's rehearsals, culminating each week in a plenary where the two halves were satisfyingly dovetailed. By and large this worked very well. Would it be as seamless when we joined forces with The Other Choir after half-term? One of my work colleagues regaled me with a dream she'd had about two choirs performing together, each having different sections to sing, and one choir responsible for about one line to the other choir's ten. Time to leave my choral anxieties at the office door, perhaps.

Shortly afterwards, I found myself in the office of David Curtis, Artistic Director of the Orchestra of the Swan in Stratford-upon-Avon. He'd kindly agreed to talk to me about the Spring Sounds International Music Festival, which would take place there in May, inspired by Tasmin Little. My idea was to compare the organisation behind a major event such as this with what we got up to in our choir. The trouble with meeting professional musicians is that I always end up wishing to be a part of that circle, rather than dabbling in music as an amateur. Not that you get a fancy office, necessarily –

David's was very modest, the small space housing the all-important fridge and kettle and dominated by a wall of bookshelves, featuring several volumes of 'Music in Shakespeare'. The remaining walls advertised OOTS' forthcoming concerts, on their trademark posters; stylish, bold and modern with clear white print leaping off a black background, and each showcasing in relaxed pose a different performer. David turned out to be as approachable in real life as the character portrayed by his photo, and as the conversation progressed, this accessibility emerged as something of a theme.

Of prime importance was the communication of passion for the music, whatever that music might be. 'We don't book people who don't smile', said David, emphasising their user-friendliness, 'or at least we don't book them twice!' Like us in the choir, the orchestra's imminent programme would celebrate significant musical anniversaries, but their approach to this was rather creative and refreshing, in no sense being hide-bound by them. With a reputation for championing and commissioning new works and encouraging contemporary composers, they manage to achieve a mix of the old and the new with some clever programming. David referred to a three-year cycle in celebration of the work of Tippett, for example. The first year didn't feature any Tippett music at all, but focused on composers who'd influenced him. Tippett's own music formed the backbone of performances in the second year, then the third year demonstrated how he in turn had influenced the younger generation of composers. Thus the orchestra's audiences – and like the choir, they tend to have their 'regulars' – are exposed to more modern repertoire that they might not otherwise be tempted to dip into. This can only make for an enriched musical experience, without audience members having to be too actively adventurous in their choices. 'A sensible context for the unaccustomed listener', was how David put it.

Spring Sounds, as well as highlighting this year's Haydn and Mendelssohn anniversaries, would provide a platform for new works from Joe Cutler, Param Vir and Roxanna Panufnik – the latter's *Tibetan Winter* being the second of her four seasons suite. Not so appropriate for the time of year, perhaps, but *Japanese Spring* had already sprung at last year's inaugural festival!

The timing of the festival in spring occurred as something of an extension to the local celebrations for Shakespeare's birthday. David revealed Tasmin's family connection with Stratford, her actor father having met her mother there, working at the theatre box office. When I asked David if he could pinpoint anything akin to a mission statement for the festival, he leant back thoughtfully in his chair, hands behind his head, and toyed with themes around celebrating spring, renewal and simply being alive. In the end he plumped for 'Come along and have a great time!' Any musical endeavour, professional or amateur, could surely emulate those sentiments. Not to mention the simplicity of Tasmin's philosophy, as quoted by David from a press interview. When asked 'What's been your greatest achievement so far?' and 'What would you like to achieve in the future?' her responses, respectively, were 'Making music with old friends' and 'Making music with new friends'. Inspired, it occurred to me that after half-term, when we were joined by The Other Choir, we'd be doing both simultaneously.

Before that, of course, we had to make direct contact with them to begin to crack on with the practical arrangements. I can't say this went as well as I would have hoped. The more people who are involved in an enterprise, the more unwieldy it can be, so we decided to convene an inner circle of the two Chairmen and those responsible for marketing and concert management in each choir. Scheduling a meeting between six people, with the three of us giving the others a range of possible dates to collectively choose from shouldn't be too difficult, surely? A week, many emails and several phone messages later, I was still trying to glean their responses, which only seemed possible on an individual basis. Did they not communicate with each other? It didn't bode well for teamworking. Finally it became obvious that if we waited for a unanimously mutually convenient date, the concert would be over, so we held a lopsided meeting with myself, the VC with his marketing hat on, the CM, and just the one delegate from The Other Choir, their publicity expert (the PE). Getting the publicity machine moving was priority number one, after all.

We agreed to meet on neutral territory, The Mermaid, although to be fair this was fast becoming our Committee's second home. We drew the line at carrying copies of *The Creation* for identification. It has to be said that we three looked much more stereotypically 'the choral singing sort', the PE being refreshingly younger for a start. Introductions were made, drinks were ordered. So far, so good. In a bid to find a suitable way forward, both sides had brought examples of their previous posters, tickets and programmes. The PE appeared not only a very creative soul but also eager to take on production of these important elements. In a spirit of fostering involvement and easing our own workload, we readily agreed to this. I had become so overwhelmed by the shenanigans to date that I even delegated to the VC and CM (and the MD if he wished) the choice between the style options the PE would produce, together with the proofreading process. As will become clear in the next couple of chapters, I didn't stick to this, of course.

'What ticket price do we put on the posters?' asked the PE as we got down to the nitty-gritty, then metaphorically threw up her hands in horror when I quoted £12. 'Our audience would never pay that much ... oh, and by the way, we always write to all the schools, offering free tickets.'

A Treasurer-shaped genie on my shoulder whispered in my ear: 'Stick to your guns, the ticket price has already been agreed by both sides of the GB, otherwise we wouldn't have a viable concert and you wouldn't be having this conversation. Freebies aren't up for discussion – we need every seat filled by a paying customer.' Hadn't this message got through to The Other Choir's committee?

Taking these concerns into account, was it a total error of judgment on my part to allow the VC's carefully prepared publicity strategy to be deposited into the PE's hands? Would she be able to adhere to the schedule for press releases and could she secure us some media coverage? Was I worrying unnecessarily and shouldn't I just delegate with dignity and get back to enjoying the music? In fact, I could identify with the sentiments unwittingly expressed during an early rehearsal, when the choir apparently made something of a hash of one of the opening phrases. *'And God said ...'* was ironically punctuated with *'STOP!'* Indeed.

Meanwhile, we pressed on with learning the notes. And words. For a meaningful performance, the audience needs to be serenaded not only with beautiful music but also intelligible lyrics. When you're dealing with a choir of 150 voices, precision is everything, especially with strategic consonants, none more so than our old friend, the terminal 's'. I've yet to meet a choral director who doesn't home in on this slippery customer, and our own MD is no exception. Like a modern-day St Patrick, he had his work cut out eliminating a multitude of hissing serpents from the movement *Awake the harp,* with its complicated fugue subject *For he both heaven and earth has clothed in stately dress.* Some of the recurring dresses were meant to be dotted crotchets, come crotchets and some mere quavers. 'Shorten your dress!' became a familiar cry when some poor soul carried the 's' through the rest. I hoped against hope that this wouldn't lead to premature discussion about concert attire.

Maybe if the 's' remained problematical we should be a little creative with the text. After all, the music publishers Novello had for reasons best known to themselves played fast and loose with Haydn's time signature in the very first choral movement *In the beginning.* They'd changed it from 2/2 to 4/4, but having a feel for our sung phrases in the original made for a much more stylish rhythm and conveyed the meaning of the words with greater musicality. Maybe we'd be forgiven, then, for messing with Milton and changing dress to frock? 'K', quite rightly, is one of the most vital consonants in choral music and can have terrific impact if delivered unanimously. 'F', on the other hand, had already come in for a bit of stick for its role in the aforementioned phrase *For he both, etc, etc.* So that it didn't disappear into oblivion, we were urged to anticipate the 'f' just before each entry, involving preparation of lungs and lips. Over and over again we practised this, section by section and then finally together, the phrases falling fast and furious. Formidable. I half anticipated the MD saying 'sorry about the f in for', but f-fortunately he didn't.

When the opportunity arose to take part in a BBC Songs of Praise recording in celebration of Handel's *Messiah,* I jumped at the chance, along with many others from the choir. I think they fancied being on the telly. For me, in my year of trying to cram in as many musical experiences as possible, a free event like this was literally a gift. Mind you, we paid for it in time commitment. A Thursday evening of solid rehearsal was followed by a 7-hour practice and recording session on the Saturday. Coming just after the Christmas/New Year lull and coinciding with the first week back at both choir and work, this could perhaps be classed as shock therapy.

But, like a tuning fork, it was two pronged in its effectiveness: it gave a fascinating insight into how such programmes are made, and singing with a thousand others in Town Hall Birmingham couldn't fail to be uplifting.

There was the same excitement and buzz at both the evening rehearsal and the day recording, but the setting was a bit different. On Thursday the stage was in a state of preparation, with piles of wires on the bare surfaces, like snakes waiting to pounce on anyone who got their notes wrong, and a distinct lack of lighting. Somebody quipped that the conductor, Paul Leddington Wright, needed white gloves for visibility. A half-hour or so into the proceedings, somebody technical must have located the correct switch ... 'and there was light'. Oh no, sorry, that's Haydn's *Creation.*

On Saturday, of course, sophisticated lighting came into play with knobs on, to bring this lovely building to life for the cameras. Subtly-changing coloured effects from below highlighted the glorious patterns on the organ pipes, and spotlights beamed on soloists and presenters. Stage choirs on blue choir benches now flanked organist Thomas Trotter, the black outfits of the adults relieved by the vibrant red of the schoolgirls' blouses. During a brief comfort break in the afternoon, several of this balcony contingent casually stood leaning against the rail overlooking the stage below, looking as though they were about to set sail. This image wasn't lost on presenter Aled Jones, who was tempted to do a Titanic double-act with composer Howard Goodall, with whom he was supposed to be analysing the history, appeal and popularity of *Messiah.* The producer had asked the massed choirs – that is, us in the stall and circle (or mantelpiece, as Paul put it, making me feel like a prized family photo) – to wear something bright and beautiful. Not only does this tend to work better on camera, but since transmission would be at Easter, we needed to look as though we hadn't just walked in off the snowy streets!

Obviously we needed to sound good, but we also got constant reminders of the visual impact we needed to create. The exhortation to sparkle and fizz with joy and excitement made perfect sense in the context of trying to engage with an imagined television audience, but the sentiments were equally transferable to any performance. Perhaps that would be the key to communication in our own choir concerts – imagine the cameras are on us. I noticed that one of the ladies in the stage choir had a tendency to throw her head around while singing, and wondered whether the TV cameras would focus on her, interpreting this irritating habit as 'joyful enthusiasm.' Looking dynamic wasn't just confined to when we were actually singing, either. The camera could be on anyone at any time! 'During the cadence, don't straighten your glasses or fluff your hair', Paul said, 'and keep perfectly still at the end'. Even during the solos and the chat sessions, we needed to at least 'pretend to be interested' for the benefit of the cameras. Not much pretence was required, as the soloists were first class and the chat fascinating, if a little repetitive while they did several takes.

The disjointed nature gave rise to several comedy moments. Flowers were 'mock' presented and then immediately claimed back. Aled came out with comments applauding the soloists, such as 'Thank you, that was absolutely wonderful', although nobody had sung a note. He and tenor Rhys Meirion plunged headlong into an interview in Welsh before noticing that the rest of us were clueless. They should perhaps have stuck to their mother tongue, though, when introducing *Thy rebuke hath broken his heart,* which for several 'takes' came out as *Thy heart hath broken his rebuke.* By and large everyone was expert at standing 'on their spot like true professionals' but there were other 'out-take' moments when they forgot what came next.

The presenters threw in some lighthearted banter about the enduring appeal of 'catchy tunes' – ones that, try as you might, you can't get out of your head. 'Like *Walking in the air,* perhaps?' teased Howard, referring to choirboy Aled's rise to fame. Aled quickly got his own back by humming Howard's *Vicar of Dibley* theme tune. When they got back to being serious, their analysis included the history of the tradition that gets everyone to their feet for the Halleluja Chorus. Allegedly this came about because King George II was so impressed by this movement that he rose from his seat and all his subjects were of course obliged to do the same. This is possibly just popular folklore, but the habit's stuck. Familiar in principle, this favourite actually has its tricky variations and vagaries, so when Paul announced he'd like us to attempt recording it without scores, a buzz of apprehension filled the Hall. A couple of practice runs gave us confidence before the real thing. Our entries were more or less spot-on, and as my fellow-soprano Sheila put it afterwards, the Lord reigned in the right place. If the tingling down the spine and almost hyperventilating with effort was anything to go by, the impact on screen would be magical. The producer was pretty impressed. Never mind all the visible trappings of 21st century technology, she rang through from the outside broadcast van to the clunky big telephone on Paul's music stand. 'Deal or no deal?' we all wondered. 'You are the last choir standing!' said our brave conductor.

It was all very well taking on these extra choral activities, but when was I going to learn all my music theory? Good intentions forged during the leisure of the Christmas holidays were in danger of turning into panic in the cruel light of an action-packed term. I'd expected the exam to be just before Easter. But 'March the 5th,' confirmed the PT, giving me barely two months to learn all the rules and regulations and try them out on a pile of practice papers. For the most part, I soaked it up, fascinated that the process was enriching my appreciation for the practical side of my music-making. Relating it to real music was a bonus, and I was consciously developing a more critical eye and ear. There was even a direct quote from *The Creation* in ET's explanations about cadences. Apparently the famous line *The heavens are telling the glory of God* is a fine example of a female cadence, the melody ending as it does on the weaker beat. I wasn't sure that did much for equal opportunities.

Dealing with the concept of transposing music wasn't too taxing, either, even though the exercises were certainly time-consuming. The idea of certain orchestral instruments needing to have their music transposed because what you saw wasn't what you got had been brought to my attention in Jasper Rees' hilarious memoir *I found my horn*. This in turn had been brought to my attention by one of my writing tutors, who'd heard it serialised on the radio. 'It's about this guy turning to music to deal with his mid-life crisis. Beautifully written. It reminds me of yours.' Did she mean it brought to mind my writing style or my mid-life crisis? The one thing that did put the frighteners on me, though, was The Melody Composition. The PT found my first attempts underwhelming. So much for finding the old exercises dull, where you had to complete a rhythm but without such niceties as having a stab at a tune. Now rhythm, melody, articulation, expression, tempo all had to find their way from the creative bit of my brain onto the manuscript paper. And all in a way that would suit a given poem. OK, it only needed to be eight bars, but there wouldn't be a handy piano sitting alongside my exam desk to try it out on. It counted for 15 marks of the 100, so it was at least worth conquering the basic principles. As far as I could gather, the most basic principle of all was 'keep it simple'. Never mind what Haydn did with his oratorios, stick to one note per syllable and approach minor keys with caution, even if the words are sad. Or, maybe safer still, avoid the exercise with the words altogether, and go for the instrumental alternative. At least that way you're given the opening bar or so, putting these two options on a less-than-equal footing in the difficulty stakes, as far as I could tell. Perversely, though, as a singer I felt drawn by a compelling magnetism towards the one with The Words.

When I got home from a particularly trying day at the office, the CC greeted me with the words 'you need cheering up then, and I've managed to get the last few tickets for the John Williams Blockbusters concert.' So instead of an evening with my theory books, I spent it in the company of the CBSO, whose playing conjured up a cast of thousands – Indiana Jones, Harry Potter, ET (the

Extra-Terrestrial, that is, not Eric Taylor), Superman, Jaws, and many other villains and heroes.

Symphony Hall was packed to the rafters. Beside me sat a gentleman with red-carpet aftershave and the breathing technique of Darth Vader. The lady in front kept shooting annoyed backwards glances. While purists might also wince at the whistling and whooping that accompanied the applause, lighthearted concerts like this give an appetising taste of a symphony orchestra to a public who might not have experienced more traditional classical music. And the music itself, combined with the alternative visual – musicians taking their cue from conductor Michael Seal, rather than actors directed by Lucas or Spielberg – was sheer entertainment. And just as dramatic.

The multi-Oscar-winning composer's output has been phenomenal by anybody's standards, and mind-blowing to someone embarking on her first simple melody compositions for Grade 5. Although there was an instantly recognisable 'signature' feel to certain pieces, there was a remarkable range of moods: excitement, menace, struggle, adventure, magic, all drawn out skilfully by the different sections of the orchestra. A very flexible keyboard player swivelled between piano, celesta and organ console, manhandling a massive score from one to another. There were no fewer than six percussionists. They – particularly the side drums – and the baker's dozen of brass instruments came into their own in the inspirational *Olympic Theme* from Munich, Saving Private Ryan's poignant *Hymn to the Fallen,* and, in the same week as the new American President's inauguration, the unmistakable patriotism of the theme to JFK.

From heart-stirring to heart-rending, CBSO Leader, Laurence Jackson, poured his soul into the haunting melodies of Schindler's List. His violin wept.

From ghostly to galactic, with the sudden unannounced invasion of a small army of Stormtroopers, Symphony Hall became a Star Wars set. Clad in light-sabre-defying white plastic from head to toe, they brandished their weapons at innocent paying customers, and even escorted Michael Seal back for his encore, hands raised not to conduct but in surrender. They were collecting money for children's charities, an irony not lost on my son, who reliably informed me that Stormtroopers are cloned. Even more suspiciously, one of them appeared to be heavily pregnant.

Maybe I needed to adopt some metaphorical body-armour, as chairing the choir was a question of confidence, I suppose. I was still so new in this role that it was remarkably difficult to feel in control as Chairman with external factors having such an effect. Even as we were trying to get to grips with getting the combined show on the road, I was fed with news of the GB's continuing discussions about permanent amalgamation. They were on the point of completing their official report for the Committee's detailed consideration, and this would mean a dedicated Committee meeting with the GB present, in a more confidential location than a public house. On my birthday. When I received a draft copy, I was very impressed by how thoroughly they'd researched all the pros, cons and legalities of the various options that would be open to the choirs, from staying totally separate to all-out merger, and a range of variations in between. It was essentially a consultative document, not designed to make recommendations, but, possibly influenced by previous email correspondence, I couldn't help reading into it an element of favouring eventual merger. Which clearly wouldn't be straightforward, including such issues as disbandment of the existing charities and transfer of assets and resources into a newly-formed one.

Indeed, the ramifications were such that if it went ahead I'd be likely to find my position untenable as I just wouldn't have the time or will to see it through, and I'd feel compelled to resign. I knew how much that would dent my self-esteem and sadden me for what might have been, so this was possibly my darkest hour. Where's *Let there be light* when you need it?

February
A decent interval

Let there be 'white', more like. I opened the curtains on 2nd February to another year of my life and to a landscape plastered with snow. All very beautiful, but what chance of a rehearsal that evening, or the all-important Committee meeting? If I'm not much mistaken, our rare snowfalls have adopted the vindictive habit of descending on a Monday, causing choral disruption galore. The decision to cancel the rehearsal was quickly taken for us, as the school would be closed. Pity really. In my naïveté I'd harboured the hope that, with my birthday falling on a Monday (rather like the snow), the choir might have made a fuss of me. It's definitely time I started acting my age.

Taking all sorts of time factors into account, I decided to aim to have the meeting anyway, depending on how conditions progressed throughout the day. The rest of the day (apart from an unscheduled lunch invitation from the CC, elated as his school was also closed) seemed to be one long round of emails and phone calls to ensure that the Committee was kept up to date, until finally letting everyone know the meeting was cancelled after all because it would just be too treacherous to get everyone out on the road. Yet more emails (with copies to be posted to the few Committee members not on email) to explain how we'd get round this non-meeting. Although I was only too aware that the GB were very keen to have face-to-face discussions to thrash out the issues and agree next steps, we were fast running out of time before half-term, after which attention would be devoted entirely to the *Creation* concert. So I invited everyone, via a painstakingly worded message, to put their views about the report and their preferred option in writing by the following week, and these would be collated and circulated amongst the Committee. If a clear way forward emerged, Hallelujah, but if not, maybe I'd disappear into the nearest snowdrift.

The following day the MD said he hoped my birthday was fun, 'free evening' and all. Aside from being one of my most frustrating ever, listing the innumerable emails, decisions, phone calls, I signed off with 'I'd rather have been singing, believe me.' Salt in the wound followed as he wanted me to check whether we might, unusually, hold a rehearsal in half-term, to make up for the missed one. No problems organisationally, just the Chairman's nose put further out of joint as she'd be unavailable to attend, having an appointment with a Swiss alp.

Back online to communicate the extra rehearsal to the general membership. I also took the opportunity to impart the practical arrangements the MD, the VC, the SM and I had agreed for the joint rehearsals. Anyone who sings in a choir will recognise the compulsion to sit in roughly the same place week by week. With a view to instant integration but without causing complete separation from familiar neighbours, there'd be interspersed clusters of labelled seats for members of The Other Choir, and a small welcoming party would ensure they were made to feel at home as quickly as possible so we could get on with the important business of the music without delay. Everyone asked to exercise some flexibility in the seating arrangements. The Other Choir's management welcomed our thoughtfulness and everything was set, even down to name labels that the Membership Secretaries of both choirs would distribute at the start.

Amongst the plaudits for these initiatives, however, stood out a complaining message. 'Do we really need to be this regimented? Surely as adults we're all capable of working out where to sit!' Resisting the urge to say that at times I'd rather manage a kindergarten, I responded that while everyone has their own way of being in charge, mine was to be prepared and not just hope for the best. 'Well, I for one won't be wearing a name badge.' I didn't dignify that one with a response.

Time for another diversion into different singing territory, as I'd signed up for a day workshop with Midlands Chorale. Hoping to be transported away from my own choral anxieties, I was however greeted by a bizarre anecdote from the VC, who was also taking part. Before leaving home, he'd answered the phone, to hear someone demanding, 'Is that *Creations*?' 'Could be,' he felt like saying, but instead discovered the caller was looking for a florist whose number was just one digit away from his own. Watch out for more on phone numbers later.

One of the simplest, but sometimes most revealing aspects of working with a different choral director is their approach to the warm-up. Coming as it inevitably does at the start of a session, it immediately gives you a glimpse of the person you're dealing with. Will they be particularly fussy about pitch? Breathing? Diction? Will they capture the attention of the assembled masses and show promise of an inspirational occasion? Or will there be something that instantly irritates you and leaves you wondering whether you could make a dash for the door during the D major scale?

If I was expecting total sobriety for the warm-up at a workshop on Rachmaninov's *Vespers*, a sublime liturgical piece, I couldn't have been more mistaken. Sure enough, director Richard Laing did start us off with a series of arpeggios, with a particular emphasis on gradually increasing and decreasing the volume. His exquisitely formed Italian vowels in *crescendo* and *diminuendo* got me on side straight away, incidentally. But then we found ourselves blasting our way unceremoniously through a rendition of *A boy had a ping pong ball* to the tune of the Lone Ranger – or, to inject at least a semblance of classical music into such tongue-twisting irreverence, Rossini's *William Tell Overture.* It was lively, it was fun, it was chaotic, but above all it got us moving our mouths, which was after all the serious purpose behind the lighthearted approach.

We should have been ready then to get cracking on the task in hand, but a few people found they needed to change places. If I ever turn up to a choral gathering where everyone is totally satisfied with their position, I expect I'll be wearing angel's wings and carrying a harp. Wouldn't that impress the Welsh in-laws? There would be further shifting during the course of the day, as the sun cast Damascene shafts of light through successive windows, the lighting in the shabby chic theatre of the public school not really being adequate for all the curtains to be shut.

On top of helping us to grapple with the notes, Richard steered us towards musicality, helping us to bring the piece alive with dynamics, but not necessarily with the greatest decorum. In a piece such as this, there's an inevitable smattering of *Alleluias,* and to shape the word we were urged to lean on the *lu.* Sniggers all round. Richard was fairly handy with encouraging compliments here and there, even if they were occasionally a bit backhanded: 'It sounds better than it looks – you look really miserable.' Someone had the temerity to leave their mobile phone on, and when it rang, Richard piped up 'If that's Rachmaninov, tell him I'm doing my best.'

I'd joined the workshop for a couple of reasons. Although I didn't know the whole work, our choir had sung the *Ave Maria* movement, which was so gorgeously ethereal that I was tempted to try the rest. And I hoped it would be useful preparation for an ambitious residential weekend in the summer, which would include parts of the *Vespers*, plus other Russian and Hungarian music – in the original language! Today's offering was in English translation, but getting to grips with some of the music seemed like a steppe in the right direction.

Although popularly known as the *Vespers,* it's more correctly entitled the *All Night Vigil,* comprising fifteen anthems that would have been interspersed with prayers and readings. Rachmaninov wrote the whole piece in about a fortnight in 1915, effectively the swansong for religious music in Russia. He based it on old chants, many written originally in strange notation from the Znamen tradition. Part of its charm, but also challenge, for singers is that it's performed *a cappella*, which stems from musical instruments being prohibited in the orthodox church. The hypnotic *Nunc Dimittis* was like a lullaby. It was apparently Rachmaninov's favourite movement and he'd requested for it to be played at his funeral although sadly this didn't happen. On a lighter note, and as an indication of the richness of Russian voices, he dismissed critics who wondered where on earth he'd find basses – 'as rare as asparagus at Christmas' – who could sing all the way down to bottom B flat.

It seemed especially appropriate to be surrounded by our own unaccustomed snowy landscape as we learned a little of the history of the piece. But still the sun did its best to play havoc with reading our scores or watching the conductor. When it came to the *Great Doxology*, which was traditionally timed to coincide with sunrise, I could certainly identify with those early 20th century Russians. A brilliant beam of white light eclipsed all vision, forcing reliance on the ears – no bad thing. Such inspirational moments, coupled with the sheer beauty of the music, almost relegated my own choral concerns to the back of my mind. Almost, but not quite. At the end of the day, there was the inevitable invitation to join the Chorale 'because we'd like to expand'. I glanced over to the basses to catch the eye of the VC. An invisible thought bubble hung between us: 'be careful what you wish for.'

Back to the real world, the Committee's responses to the GB report didn't yield too many surprises. Everyone was keen to acknowledge the significant pitfalls of amalgamation, particularly those that increased size would generate. How would it affect our choice of concert venues? How would it affect our choice of concert repertoire? How would it affect our sense of identity? However, the magnetism of singing in a huge crowd can exercise a strong pull and some were broadly in favour. The snowdrifts had melted by now, so I had to face reality and admit that without a direct, unanimous steer from the Committee, we'd be looking at taking the issue to the vote at an Extraordinary General Meeting. But the business of rehearsing and performing together hadn't even been attended to at this point, and I urged my colleagues to wait and see. Like a well-practised pianist, I crossed my fingers in all the right places that it would be a triumph musically. Organisationally, I wasn't so optimistic.

Nor was I hugely optimistic about my chances with music theory, as all this choral chaos took up time I might have spent revising. I took to scrutinising the *Creation* score more closely during rehearsals, to test out my new-found knowledge. While the altos were being drilled in a passage from *By thee with bliss,* I spotted an unusual-looking interval in the line we were about to tackle: *Ye creatures all, extol the Lord* (ending on A flat), then up to F sharp for *Him celebrate, him magnify,* and concentrated on working it out. The next moment, the MD was saying, 'This is a tricky interval coming up for the sops, does anyone happen to know what it is?' 'An augmented 6th?' I ventured without hesitation. I don't know who was more shocked, him that I knew the answer or me that he'd read my mind. It bore all the hallmarks of a set-up, of course, but I didn't care as it gave me an extra confidence boost, convincing me that I finally understood intervals well enough to identify them without the benefit of a keyboard in front of me. Identifying them, though, was one thing. Singing them quite another.

Wherever I go on holiday, I always count it a bonus if I encounter some music either by design or chance, so I hoped the Swiss might oblige in my year of living musically. After all, on a previous visit, there'd been a wonderful baroque chamber ensemble playing in the tiny local church, with the musicians togged up in curly wigs and knee breeches. Earlier in the day, I'd seen them arriving by anachronistic cable car, harp and all. This time, though, I had to content myself with my theory practice papers and the music of the natural world. While the rest of the family went skiing, I'd take myself for solitary walks. Wandering through forests with fir trees so tall that they seemed to be propping up the sky, or along paths bordered by swathes of snow like diamond-encrusted silk, maybe you'd think there'd be just silence. Especially as there was an almost complete absence of people. But the self-imposed isolation heightened all my senses, so that not only was I immersed in the beauty of the visuals, the light slanting smokily through the trees, the mountain peaks so clear across the valley that it felt like I could reach out and touch them, but nature's orchestra provided the soundtrack.

The rhythm was established by my marching boots, as the snow crunched steadily underfoot. The score might read *rubato*, though, as such military precision was of necessity allowed a certain freedom here and there, where the snow was less crisp and even. Deep it certainly was, following 16 hours' solid snowfall. But now that the warming sun shone again, the overloaded branches began to shed their icing sugar burdens, avalanching veils of snow from time to time. That harp would have been useful to capture the effect as the snow filtered through the gigantic trees, but as it finally plummeted to the ground with a dull thud the spotlight would turn to the timpani. There was a distant *vibrato* hum of a ski tow. The trees creaked and tapped percussively, a sound that echoed in the stillness. My heart was anything but still, the aerobic exercise making its pounding beat virtually audible to my ears as those marching feet trudged on, with just the slightest hint of a *rallentando*. Well, why rush, I was on holiday after all?

Back to choir, and if only everything could have gone as smoothly as that first joint rehearsal. Almost everyone was on their best behaviour, nobody seemed upset by sitting in a slightly different place from usual, and introductions went well. 'Wow!' I said, surveying the scene as I climbed onto the podium to welcome our guests. 'I've only just got used to addressing a room full of a hundred people, and now there's half as many again!' Most importantly our combined voices immediately worked harmoniously. In fact the extra fullness and richness of sound was instantly invigorating.

I reminded myself that this was what it had to be all about.

After a preliminary 'My, haven't you grown?' the MD got into his stride, soon abandoning the odd layer of clothing and rolling up his shirt sleeves well before we got anywhere near the stately dress.

Normally straight after half term we'd be dishing out posters and tickets in a bid to muster a fine audience, but there was an inexplicable delay. I'd made some initial comments to my own team on the suggested poster styles, since they were copied to me, and it would have been out of character for me to keep my opinions completely to myself. Then I left it to them to sort out which choir name came first (who was running this show, by the way?), decide whether the curly writing was actually legible to someone who didn't know what it said already, ensure the soprano soloist's name was spelled correctly, and include the name of the city rather than just the name of the church, since posters would be displayed further afield. Not only did all these aspects remain incorrect on the finished article, but it turned out that the final '0' on the Box Office telephone number had mysteriously dropped off between the proof stage and the printers. This wasn't deemed too catastrophic, apparently, as 'not many tickets are sold through the Box Office anyway'. I wonder why. As Ronnie Barker might have said, 'Got any 0s?' I fell to musing whether, for the sake of consistency, I should suggest we miss out an odd '0'-shaped semibreve here and there from the music. The CC kindly delivered one of the posters to our local library. 'Not very easy to read, is it?' said the Librarian. 'It's a long story,' said the CC.

No sooner were our joint rehearsals underway than I went off to sing with another bunch of strangers.

The 'Sing!' event from the Royal College of Organists commemorated no fewer than four composers with noteworthy dates: 200 years since the death of Haydn and the birth of Mendelssohn, 250 years since the death of Handel, and 350 years since the birth of Purcell.

The sense of history was underlined when I compared notes with my neighbour, Hilary, who'd travelled up to Manchester Cathedral from Buckinghamshire. Whereas I'd downloaded my scores from the internet, hers were yellowing copies that bore price labels such as '2d'. It didn't escape my sense of irony that Joseph Cullen, our conductor for the day, was very fond of the phrase 'in the old money', delivered in a gentle Scots lilt, when directing us to certain bars or pages. Hilary's *Zadok the Priest* (well, Handel's, actually) proudly sat within a soft red-bound edition of the complete Coronation Service from 1953. It had belonged to her grandfather, who incidentally had celebrated his Golden Wedding on Coronation day. Hilary's husband, Geoff, had a deluxe hard-back copy of the Coronation Service which cost the princely sum of 8/6 – for those of you born since 1971, this equates to 42.5p!

Whether our copies were hot off the computer or treasured family heirlooms, the music remained constant, and in any case we were encouraged not to look down at it but to sing out. Surrounded by history as evidenced by bomb-damaged walls contrasted with modern stained glass, around 150 voices of all ages joined forces. The Cathedral's pillars got in the way a bit, but otherwise there were no barriers.

In Purcell's *Thou knowest, Lord, the secrets of our hearts*, Joseph drew attention to the gaps in the music. In a bid for precision, we needed to be careful 'not to let the bricks crumble' when there was just a brief rest (the mortar) between two blocks of singing – but equally we needed to make sure the gaps were there.

It's just such emphasis on style and detail that helps participants at these events bring singing to life. In Mendelssohn's *Hear my prayer* Joseph exhorted us to deliver textual energy and commitment, transmitting the words with face, soul and heart, and this included practical considerations such as not letting our heads jump when the music jumped up an octave! There was a rare foray into discussing pitch when he encouraged us to use 'effort and fuel' when repeating the same note, for fear it would all go downhill, but most coaching revolved around dynamics – 'exercise some choral charity, don't knock the soprano soloist over!' – stance, demeanour, rhythm – ' there's an imaginary timpanist behind you, helping you keep time' – mood, breathing – 'there are too many commas in poetry' – and diction – in Haydn's *Nelson Mass* we were to exercise 'fast mouths' to convey a more continental flavour to the Latin words.

The real star of the show was the organ, which under Christopher Stokes' expert hands and feet did the work of an entire orchestra. He might have been out of sight up in his loft, but we didn't mind the gap.

March
That's the theory

Nor was there any discernible gap musically between the two choirs, as we pressed on as one body of singers. The greater numbers seemed to lend us confidence, not only to sing out when required but also to hold back and add the subtleties that give choral singing its stylish light and shade, and which help to tell the story. It was at this point that we could strive for some polish, the sort of thing that can turn a satisfactory performance into an unforgettable one. We laboured for precision in the length of notes, observing the rests accurately, enunciating our vowels and diphthongs correctly and our consonants clearly and unanimously. We practised breathing silently. We grappled with the words, shaping and phrasing to draw out the meaning. What we were effectively trying to do was breathe air into the music, like some higher being giving life to his creation.

With the notes and dynamics reasonably well mastered, the MD's next tactic was to aim for a stronger connection with him – and hence to the audience – by urging us to learn certain passages off by heart. An audience doesn't want to see the tops of people's heads, after all, even if freshly-coiffed. They want to see enthusiastic faces. The results ranged from chaotic to amusing at first, and it has to be said there was the odd furtive glance at a copy here and there, when all eyes were supposed to be on the maestro. But we were emboldened by a few attempts, and stunned by the difference it made to the sound's impact. We kept more unanimously to the beat; we could follow every nuance of the MD's hands and face; we were more aware of the other parts and how we all fitted together; we did fit together because we saw our cues and got our entries right. This was as opposed to the times when we didn't look up sufficiently, with the unfortunate consequence that everyone attempted to go at their own speed. The MD was inordinately pleased with himself one evening, hitting upon the analogy of steering an ocean liner when we weren't quite as responsive as his frantic arms demanded. Perhaps the Titanic Choir would be a suitable moniker for the proposed super-sized Society?

I was more than happy to have a go at this looking up lark, as I felt the dots and dashes on the page had become as familiar to me as every twist and dip on my commute, accompanied at it always was by my well-worn CD. So what if the occasional driver in front thought he was being followed by a wailing banshee if he risked an eye in his rear-view mirror? I discovered by accident – no, not an accident on the road, surprisingly enough – that the best way of testing how well one knows the music is to arrive at rehearsal having forgotten ones glasses. That particular evening, the score, as far as I was concerned, might just as well have read 'Musicians United, five; Singing City, nil', so I abandoned the book altogether. It was one of the most liberating experiences ever, with an undeniable moral: you do know it well enough – go for it and don't look down!

Which is not to say 'Don't look back', and this is what I did when I treated myself to a visit to my old University. The Great Hall was smaller than I remembered. But then the grandeur of graduation three decades ago was probably a factor. The reminiscences of a gentleman named Jim, sitting next to me, went back even further. Sixty years ago he'd studied medicine, but he'd been given special permission to play the organ from time to time, after watching it being built, its constituent parts carried in, pipe by pipe.

I'd been tempted back to Bristol in centenary year to hear top-ranking organist Jennifer Bate OBE, who had both an undergraduate and honorary degree from the University, expounding through words and music on the subject 'The organ – box of whistles or king of instruments?' Mozart's quote was a perfect title for the whistle-stop tour through the complexities and mechanics of the instrument's components, delivered with gentle humour and just the right combination of plain English and technical detail. Our voyage of discovery was illustrated by excerpts from relevant pieces, either on the Great Hall organ or via recordings on historic instruments.

We were introduced to 'families' of sound, each with members of varying sizes – flutes ranging from 1' to 32', for example – sounded by means of numerous stops and pedals. Further orchestral imitations emanated from pipes termed strings, cornets and reeds, the latter including, incongruously, the trumpet. I'll admit to getting a bit lost when it came to diapasons, mutations and mixtures, but it was fascinating nevertheless.

Clever camerawork meant that giant screens gave the enthusiastic audience simultaneous close up views of the musician's busy hands and feet. Jennifer may prefer to practise in worn-out shoes, for a better feel for the pedals, but in performance her footwear was stunning: soft black leather with silver bows and heels (low ones, of course). If there'd been an audience poll for the most popular piece, I suspect George Thalben-Ball's *Variations on a Theme of Paganini* would have won hands down – a thrilling example of music expertly played with pedals only, incorporating an amazingly versatile range of sounds, dynamics and colours, my own favourite being an exciting glissando and staccato combination. Organ music staid? I don't think so!

We were allowed a glimpse of the virtuoso's private side, as she spoke affectionately of her upbringing in a musical family, including her mother who considered the organ 'unladylike'! A question from the floor about the instruments Jennifer had played over the years heralded a perfect cadence to the proceedings. She's never put off by an instrument's deficiencies, since the music itself is paramount and she does her utmost to coax it out of the most recalcitrant box of whistles.

As well as the musical enrichment, it was a real treat to revisit old haunts and revive memories. Many things had changed and developed in the intervening years, of course. I went to eat at Brown's, which I didn't recall from student days. I thought of asking one of the waiters whether it had been there then, until I realised that none of them would even have been born that far back. It was with the wisdom of my years, then, that I watched students traipsing up the hill the following morning to their 9 o'clock lectures, with their whole lives ahead of them, as I sat over a leisurely breakfast. Student loans, exams, assignments notwithstanding, I felt like shouting out of the window 'Do you realise how lucky you are?'

No sooner back from all this student reminiscence, than it was time for The Theory Exam. No, honestly, it really is possible to write something entertaining about a theory exam, so please don't fast forward to the next chapter. I felt well prepared and was comforted by the fact there'd be no performance involved, so it didn't faze me to take my place in a room full of eight-year-olds. What put me off straight away, though, was the meagre allowance of rough paper. The invigilator's preamble made it plain that we weren't to use anything other than the A5 sheet of manuscript paper provided for our rough notes or workings-out.

Manuscript paper, with its printed staves, is of course very useful in practising writing out any music and would be invaluable for the infamous melody composition, but since I'd become very attuned to plotting out my grid of key signatures and scribbling a pretend keyboard on a large sheet of plain paper, this was bad news! How on earth could I decipher what I'd written or drawn with all these fiddly lines in the way? Perhaps the credit crunch was an excuse for cutting back on paper, but at an entry fee of £27.40, you'd think they could have stretched to something a little more generous. However, there was no point dwelling on this little set back as the two hours were underway and it was time to get a move on. *Accelerando,* you might say.

A quick glance through the paper revealed that one of my favourite types of question wasn't there – the one where you have to re-write a 'short-score' as 'open-score', in other words give each section in a choir their own line to read from rather than having sopranos and altos squeezed onto one and tenors and basses on the other. The main worry with such an exercise was to ensure you had the tenors singing in the correct register, rather than turning them into *castrati.* For someone involved in choral singing, there's something very satisfying about working at getting it all laid out immaculately, and barring sheer carelessness I wouldn't have dropped any marks on that.

Instead I was faced with something that hadn't featured at all in any of the dozen practice papers I'd attacked: dividing a piece of music into phrases. Fairly straightforward on the face of it, especially as the first phrase was indicated as an example. The following squiggle on the page, though, was a quaver rest – would that form part of the next phrase, or is a silence at the beginning of a phrase a contradiction in terms? There was the distinct possibility of a dropped mark or two there, and in my quest for a distinction I couldn't afford many. Full marks in the melody composition would be unlikely, since there was bound to be an element of subjectivity about that. I had a quick glance at the choice between completing a given instrumental opening and starting from scratch on setting a short verse to music. Thus Christina Rossetti's *thin swift moon* shone in the background while I tackled the 'right or wrong' answers.

The very first bar of the very first question set the heartbeat going at a faster tempo than usual. The task was to identify missing time signatures, which differed in each of three consecutive bars. It took me back to singing Vaughan Williams' *Fantasia on Christmas Carols.* Why hadn't I paid more attention then? Bars two and three didn't pose too much of a threat, the assorted dots and dashes grouped together in such a way that they totted up to a fairly convincing 3/4 and 9/8 respectively, but the mixture of semiquavers and dotted quavers in bar one was beamed together somewhat randomly, it seemed to me, and had me puzzled. Numerically, in terms of note values, it couldn't be anything other than 5/8, and this seemed quite safe, being one of the irregular time signatures introduced at Grade 5, but I had to keep going back to check, as it just looked plain odd.

Maybe it was something to do with a search for lost youth, but it was rather therapeutic sitting in the peace and quiet of the exam hall. Just occasionally there'd be the sound of fevered rubbing out or a dropped pencil. After 40 minutes – the minimum time candidates must stay in the room – there was a little flurry of activity while those who were satisfied that they couldn't improve on their offerings escaped to their waiting parents. I was determined not to leave the room until I was thrown out, even if this meant I had time to check everything six times over.

I devoted a good half-hour to the eight-bar composition. Instead of possibly the easier option of completing the given instrumental opening, I chose to write a melody for the poem, whose iambic pentameters seemed to lend themselves to a steady 3/4 time signature, with a rather boring, though hopefully safe, alternating minim and crotchet pattern. Again playing safe, I stuck it all in C major and based the shape of the melody around a series of arpeggios, observing the rules of starting the upbeat on the dominant and finishing on the tonic. The gin would have to wait. A scattering of expression marks completed Dixson's Opus No 1, including an irresistible, if risky, *crescendo ed accelerando.* Well, it was supposed to be a musical representation of a *swift moon,* after all.

Genuine composers wouldn't have anything to worry about, of course, and I wasn't too surprised to see our friend Haydn putting in an appearance in the exam paper in his anniversary year. The name of the extract we were given escapes me, but I do know that it started in C minor, finished in E flat major, and included the following: a repeat sign, an appoggiatura, a IIb - Va cadence, and it was to be played at an *Allegro con brio* tempo. So much for learning all the German expressions in the syllabus. Nor was I asked to demonstrate my knowledge of enharmonic equivalents or those wonderful augmented 6ths, although plenty of other intervals were to be identified. Thankfully I avoided calling a diminished 5th 'minor', as there's no such thing.

Having checked my clefs, double-checked my duplets, triple-checked my triplets and quadruple-checked everything else, once outside the hall I was immediately overcome by self-doubt. Had I really been asked to write out a chromatic scale? Had I misread the question and should it have been a major or minor scale instead? As it was I'd attempted it twice anyway, starting on the given C sharp and descending an octave semitone by semitone, distributing flats right, left and centre as appropriate. That looked odd as it naturally led me to a D flat and I really needed to finish back on C sharp (its enharmonic equivalent – see, Mr Examiner, I do know it), so I tackled it again using sharps instead. Although this called for a plethora of naturals as well, it felt like a more satisfactory result. Until I started doubting my ability to read the question. Could that be a further five marks down the drain? All would be revealed in six weeks, and there would doubtless be plenty to distract me in the meantime.

The greatest time-wasting distraction turned out to be a fixation on what the new choir would be called. You might think this was a case of putting the finale before the overture, since we hadn't actually yet plumped for amalgamation or non-amalgamation. Did we really want to go to the trouble of agreeing on a name, only to find we didn't merge after all? It would be a bit like spending a year of your life writing a book without the guarantee of publication at the end of it. No, that's a bad analogy in the present circumstances. Anyway, the inner circle of The Other Choir seemed to think it was a deal-breaker if we couldn't first agree on the name, rudely citing it as our choir's biggest stumbling block and falsely accusing us of reneging on our (non-existent) promise to have discussed it by now. There seemed to be no understanding of the far greater hurdles of concert-venue size and repertoire implications for an enlarged choir. Not to mention whether anyone would be daft enough to want to steer it all through the transition stage. Some rather firm emails were called for, emphasising that we'd just have to agree to differ, and that we were sticking to our original timescale for decision-making. We would decide any possible next steps – in the merger, not the name – after *The Creation*. Preferably with at least one day of rest in between.

There were more pleasurable distractions too, though, including my reunion with that most unlikely piece of kitchen furniture, the piano. Apart from a few arpeggios (kitchen scales?) and the occasional flick of a duster, I'd barely touched it while I'd been cramming theory, so it was a welcome relief to get the digits dancing again. Although a slow waltz was more achievable than a frantic polka. Gratifyingly, the stuff on the staves made rather more sense after my immersion in the world of How Music Works. I retrieved the book of Grade 6 pieces from the piano stool, with the intention of pushing my boundaries a little rather than aiming to ever present them to some poor unsuspecting examiner. There was some lovely material contained therein, including a piece by one Wilhelm Stenhammar, unimaginatively entitled *Molto tranquillo, semplice* (more a performance direction, really, but let's not quibble about names). With plenty of octave stretches and other demands upon my coverage of the keyboard, my fingers remained to be persuaded of the *semplice* bit, but with its forgiving, slow tempo and gorgeous plaintive harmonies and chord progressions, it was *tranquillo* indeed. Just the job for calming down after the occasional incoming trouble-making choir email.

Certain aspects of concert preparation went without a hitch, in the capable hands of the CM and her counterpart, including plans to minimise the squash, as it were, in the interval drinks queue. For the first time in my ten-year history with the choir, nobody batted an eyelid (sporting whatever colour of mascara, or none) when concert dress was announced. Ladies would wear black. No questions about style or sleeve-length, just 'let there be black'. And there was black. Let there be a programme; and there was a programme. Eventually. Having had my fingers burned by too freely delegating poster production, I kept a close eye on the programme – except that what I saw via email wasn't necessarily what we got, as the formatting seemed to go awry on its journey through the ether and the PE's layout ended up looking bizarre, with page breaks in all the wrong places. The straightforward errors of spelling and grammar should have been easy enough to deal with, but what was less fathomable was the insistence on keeping the print size so tiny as to be bordering on illegible, while the borders themselves were huge. On close inspection of the listing of the movements within the piece, it seemed the PE had inadvertently missed out three or four of our major choral movements. Had I missed the announcement about us omitting *The heavens are telling*, which would be akin to singing *Messiah* without the *Hallelujah Chorus?*

'No, I wanted to fit it all onto one page, so I had to leave a few bits out, and made sure I listed the more important parts – the arias.' And there was me thinking choruses were important in a choral work. Having received explicit instructions as to how she could easily spread the complete, unabridged running order over one and a half pages by rearranging the text on the previous page, the PE came up with further drafts. We arrived at a workable document in the end, but it was a disheartening process. There'd need to be some serious grovelling to our regular programme designer afterwards.

Just when I thought it was all resolved and 500 programmes would arrive on concert day, at the very end of our final Monday rehearsal my counterpart broke the news that, although he was arranging to print the programmes as agreed, somebody else would need to fold them. Nothing quite as straightforward as the neatly folded and stapled 8 sides of A5 that we normally get, then. I had to bring into play my personal folding machine, also known as my long-suffering family. Mind you, they didn't have to fold quite as many as 500, as The Other Chairman had decided in his wisdom that, following the latest ticket sales figure, he'd only bother to print 400. With 150 going to the choir, and programmes included in the ticket price, I could only assume he hoped we wouldn't get an audience of more than 250.

In the run up to a concert I'd always update the choir on progress with ticket sales. At about a fortnight before the concert, we were diabolically low, at about the equivalent of one ticket sold per choir member, which would just about cover the cost of the staging and two and a half soloists, without even starting on the orchestra. I knew for a fact that some members had sold handfuls, so clearly some weren't bothering at all. Even with the box office number corrected, we weren't doing much better there. The VC had popped in to enquire while in town, and had misheard 'sold out'. The answer was actually 'sold eight'. As our MD might have said, correct vowel sounds are so important, aren't they? By the last Monday, sales had at least gone well into the 200s, but we were banking on at least 300, so hopefully there'd be a rush on the door, even if this meant extra hassle for our hard-working Front of House helpers.

Of course, final rehearsals just wouldn't be the same without some sort of panic or technical hitch. This time the MD managed to turn up without first throwing himself into a ditch, but also without his voice. You might think conductors do nothing but wave their arms around, and that they should be seen and not heard, but in rehearsal this is far from the truth. Apart from the requisite versatility that allows them to sing every single voice part (although not necessarily at the same time), they need to point out bar numbers so we're in with a chance of everyone starting any given section in the same place, and bark instructions to minimise the odd erroneous intake of breath and other imperfections. The bark perforce turned into a valiant whisper. Sign language and some helpful interpretation by the PA – that's the Piano Accompanist, not the Public Address system – got us through this most unusual of rehearsals. The surprisingly good results were doubtless partly due to the fact that the circumstances dictated everyone should be on their best behaviour and display listening skills they didn't realise they had. If this was what it took to silence the chatterers on the back row, maybe I should ask him to lose his voice more often.

April
Tiers before bedtime

What would April be remembered for? Fools? Showers? A fabulous *Creation* concert? Television stardom? An answer to The Merger Question? All of the above, but from my point of view the starring role has to be the phone call announcing my theory result. All it lacked was a preceding drum roll. It came about two weeks earlier than anticipated, for a start, and could I in all honesty have expected the 96% that was apparently the verdict?

Coming as it did just as I was on my way out on Friday evening to help erect the concert staging for the following day, I arrived at the church brimming over with smugness, 'distinction' written across my enlarged forehead as I entered into the proceedings *con brio*. Pride, however, comes before a fall. Once the working party – some ten of the stalwarts from our choir and a welcome but numerically-challenged couple from The Other – had person-handled the first couple of layers into place, the SM called for a chair to be brought over to check the distance was correct. As I was nearest to a stray chair, I grabbed it with one hand, ratchet still in the other, and bounded up our new-created steps. And promptly tripped on the edge of one of them, landing flat on my face. So much for being 'Chair'man. Maybe it would knock some sense into me. The major casualty was my dignity, but I also sustained a grazed knee, a compressed thumb that reminded me instantly of the CC's holiday visit to Béziers hospital after a canoeing accident, and a lip that felt like a swarm of bees had been battling it out with a demented dentist to see who could inflict the most pain. I wondered whether I'd get away with a slight adjustment in my concert dress, namely a paper bag over the head.

There was little time to dwell on such trivialities, and I put behind (and below) me my close encounter with Row C as we ventured ever heavenward with ever lengthening scaffolding legs, eventually scaling the dizzying heights of Row M, towering above the altar. How fitting it might have been, in honour of the chromatic scale that must have been correct after all, to label the rows C sharp, D, D sharp, E, F, F sharp, etc. This would have been fine when ascending the stage, but on the way back down again some of the rows ought technically have sprouted natural signs, so it would all get a bit complicated, and let's face it, pretentious. Best let the SM carry on with his tried and tested systems. He made a great job of liaising with the contractor, who pointed out which bits of leg needed to go in which bits of platform. This didn't go without its hiccups, however, as the 7 inch'ers we'd inserted into Row D were deemed to be wrong and we had to remove those –giving the Chairman the opportunity to learn the new skill of reverse-ratcheting in the process – and replace with 9 inch'ers. Only to discover that we'd been right in the first place. 'Never mind, we're used to doing things over and over again in choir!' There also had to be a slight re-configuration of the original stage plan, as a crucial set of the really high legs had been left off the lorry. 'Maybe we could prop this bit up on a pile of *Creation* scores? We don't need to look at them after all!'

It was hard, hot, heavy work for three solid hours, but with a satisfying sense of teamwork and camaraderie, not unlike choral singing itself. The working party could be justly proud of the finished result. Here was proof at last, after the debate all those months ago, that there was room for every singer.

The big question now was: would the performance measure up?

When everyone gathered on the afternoon of the Big Day, there was a general sense of satisfaction with the magnificent staging and, as far as I could gather, no fighting over seats. Every single singer had a fine view of the MD, even if his usual volume hadn't quite been restored. There was a rumour of a wailing and gnashing of teeth emanating from one of The Other Choir's sopranos, stationed on the very top row, suffering from either vertigo or altitude sickness, but this turned out to be the product of someone's overactive imagination. Perhaps the SM's pre-concert health and safety announcements, which always had air hostess overtones, ought on this occasion to include instructions about oxygen masks. Luckily my stage-building injuries hadn't resulted in my face sticking out like a sore thumb, after all, and as for the sore thumb itself, well, that shouldn't affect my ability to sing as long as I could perfect a pain-free position in which to hold the score.

There's no law that says you have to rehearse everything in precise performance order, although on concert day itself this would usually be the case. This afternoon, however, was necessarily higgledy-piggledy because we were missing the bass soloist, Chris Foster, for the early part of the practice. The CM then found she'd missed a call from him, lost at the wrong church and wanting directions. Like a naughty schoolgirl, I surreptitiously passed a scribbled note to the VC, a couple of rows behind, suggesting the soloist probably been navigating by means of the city-less posters. 'Which church have you been to?' asked the MD when Chris was finally reunited with us. 'Which church *haven't* I been to?' he groaned. A ripple of relieved laughter barely gave him time to shed his coat, before we backtracked and got stuck into the first movement. I made a mental note to ask whether any of the multifarious denominations on his grand tour had presented good-sized performance facilities, preferably with in-built staging. And another mental note to ensure that our visitors are given fail-safe instructions. A word to the wise: the postcode for a church may in fact refer not to the sacred building itself but to the parish office, in this case absolutely nowhere near each other.

The afternoon rehearsal seemed dangerously short in terms of the choral bits, allowing time afterwards for the MD to put the soloists through their paces, and I for one didn't feel particularly prepared. However, there's an unwritten rule that says an uninspiring rehearsal is often followed by a correspondingly wonderful performance, and possibly vice-versa, so I hoped for the best. If nothing else, at least I had a leisurely break in which to change into the stately dress.

Choir members were under the SM's strict instructions not to assemble until 7.15pm, to allow the audience plenty of space to make their way in, but I'm ashamed to say I pulled rank and made an early entrance to satisfy myself that everything was under control. It was, thanks to a small army of Front of House staff, camp followers of both choirs, easily identifiable in yellow sashes, who efficiently sold tickets, distributed programmes and ushered people away from the door. The church was filling up gratifyingly well, upstairs as well as down, and it looked like we might be in for a record attendance. Not only good news for the balance sheet, but it's always good for the performers to enjoy a sizeable adoring public. So what if it was going to be a squash in the interval? At least it would be a squash with atmosphere.

The atmosphere was there from the first note, with fine all-round communication between choirs, conductor, orchestra, soloists and audience. There may have been an odd wrong entry or a flat note here and there, but there were also many tingling moments and a strong sense of teamwork. I felt swept along on an emotional tide of relief, excitement, pride and sheer pleasure in the music. Dispensing with the copy for large chunks, I was more aware of the visual as well as the aural impact. After the lengthy build-up, it was over all too soon, although it wouldn't be forgotten in a hurry. Together we'd created something beautiful.

Another army of helpers then had to set about un-creating the stage. I left them to it, but made a point of sending individual messages of thanks to the workforce. By rights the day following *The Creation* should have been a day of rest, but surely any Chairman worth his or her salt would do his or her best to keep morale up by showing appreciation to those who get the show on the road, in whatever role. In turn, I received a note of congratulations from the XC, who probably remembered only too well how rarely the Chairman is on the receiving end of any thanks.

There wasn't much breathing space between the thank-you-letter-writing episode and the next instalment in The Merger Debate. True to our word, once the concert was safely performed, the Committee would need to come to some agreement about what – if anything – we did next in response to The Other Choir's request for amalgamation. This meant another meeting, not only with a full turn-out of the Committee, but also the GB. Having taken advice beforehand, it was clear that we'd have to call an Extraordinary General Meeting, and quick, so that neither choir needed to keep their plans on hold for longer than could be helped.

Luckily, by this stage there was a strong sense of unanimity amongst the Committee, matched by that of the GB. While everyone had found the experience of the joint concert rewarding, getting to that point had presented too many trials and tribulations. We'd benefit from hindsight if we ventured into similar territory in the future, which could well be desirable for large-scale works, but nobody was keen to pursue a permanent merger. Nevertheless, we had to give the whole choir the opportunity to voice their opinion. We were bound by a rule in our Constitution whereby we had to give 14 days' written notice to members, and there were Bank Holiday deliveries – or lack of them – to contend with, so the HS valiantly promised to pull everything together, based on documents drafted by the GB, to post out within 48 hours, having circulated to Committee colleagues for proofreading first.

I informed The Other Chairman about what we were up to. The response from his gang – How can you conduct this vote if we haven't yet agreed a name? – didn't command much of my attention, I'm afraid.

A couple of days later, EGM notices and voting papers landed on everyone's doormats. A day or so after that, I took another look at them, thinking ahead to how we'd communicate the outcome of The Vote to The Other Choir, whichever way it went. Taking it from the top, I was horrified by the dawning realisation that everyone's proofreading had proved that you tend to read what you expect to read. Instead of our own choir name, it was headed with a title morphed from both choirs' names. Would everyone think we had already not only decided upon a merger but also agreed a new name, without any consultation? Of all the errors there might have been, this seemed the most cruelly ironic, given our resistance to being pushed into the name debate. Maybe nobody else would even have noticed? Should I leave well alone? But if they had, would somebody perhaps legitimately claim the vote was null and void if it was actually addressed to members of a non-existent organisation?

To complicate matters further, we were in the throes of some major decorating at home, which resulted in internet access being out of the question. So what might have been a quick apologetic circular to put matters straight became a special trip to the Library to go online. This in turn was further complicated by a prior journey to dispose of a load of carpet underlay and brutal gripper rods at the Council Tip, on the way back from where the car's thermostat decided to give up the ghost and I ended up with smoke billowing from under the bonnet. Some Wagner wouldn't have gone amiss. One AA man and an hour or so later, I finally made it to the Library just before closing time. Barely enough time to register a couple of incoming messages from eagle-eyed basses, confused and mock enraged (or maybe truly enraged?) by our apparent name change, and to bash out a quick round-robin:

At the risk of drawing attention to an error that might have gone unnoticed by the majority, I am writing to apologise for the confusion over choir names as quoted on the EGM papers recently circulated. Our choir name remains the same. Please be aware that the paperwork had to be prepared rather hastily in order to comply with our obligation to give 14 days' notice of the EGM, and thus this error was missed at the proofreading stage. As many of you have been kind enough to acknowledge, the Committee has been extremely busy on your behalf recently, and I trust we'll therefore be forgiven this lapse!

Easter then intervened, bringing welcome respite from merger anxieties. Not that it was a choir-free day, since it was time for the first Songs of Praise broadcast, my viewing punctuated by exhortations not to get chocolate on the new carpet. The cameras darted around rather rapidly, so most of our glimpses of familiar faces – looking up and smiling, of course – were somewhat fleeting. The one exception was the VC, who stood out several times centre-screen, advantaged by height, a red shirt and, needless to say, stunning singing. As predicted, the Hallelujah Chorus without scores, which rounded off the first show, was a triumph. Knowing when she was onto a good thing, the producer had decided to use it again to kick off the second instalment, a week later. All very well, until after the final majestic Hallelujah the cameras panned to a section of singers as they sat down, folding their books. What books?! Perhaps the continuity person had become confused by the fact that *el gran hombre de la camisa roja* – the tall man in the red shirt – was now wearing a dark jacket on top. How on earth did he manage that when it was all recorded at the same time? Whatever we looked like, it all sounded splendid and the real star of the show was the music. But it was still fun to see ourselves on the telly.

Following a day on the home front, with three loads of washing flapping in the breeze, I turned up at the Town Hall again for a Rossini concert, where a quote from the composer leapt from the pages of the programme: 'Give me a laundry list, and I'll set it to music.' I'll look out for that one in the melody exercise in my next theory paper. A foil for such boasting came in the shape of another domestic analogy from Chris Foster, who'd been our Raphael/Adam in *The Creation*, and was bass soloist in this performance of the *Petite Messe Solennelle*. When I told the CM, meeting her by chance in the bar beforehand, that Chris was singing that evening, her comment was 'Let's hope he found it!' Chris' similarly irreverent comment was 'Rossini arias are far too long in my opinion and I'd gladly take the garden shears to them!'

In truth, since performing the piece with our choir the year before, I'd forgotten just how much solo work was in it, with chunks of half an hour at a stretch when the chorus is required to do nothing but look interested and not fidget, but I'd been tempted to come and listen to the City of Birmingham Choir's version as I'd enjoyed it so much. It would be good to let someone else do all the hard work for a change. Or would I be itching to join in? Speaking of hard work, it would certainly have been a luxury to file onto the Town Hall's ready-made choir benches without the erect-it-yourself hassle. On the other hand, the choir, high above the stage on which were set two embracing pianos and a harmonium, seemed impossibly distant from the conductor and soloists. Chris confirmed afterwards that they could have done with some substantial scaffolding to compensate for the height differential and that he and the tenor, in turn, also felt laterally removed from the soprano and contralto, but thankfully for the audience the combined sound did work. Squashed though we often feel in our concert venues, this perhaps creates an atmosphere of intimacy which adds to the warmth (sometimes literally!) of a performance.

Immodest though Rossini might have been, he did know how to write a good tune. Far from the suggested solemnity of the title, the piano music goes bounding along and wouldn't be out of place as the soundtrack to a silent movie depicting stripy-jumpered villains chased by truncheon-wielding policemen. Fiendishly difficult to play, I would imagine, and I wondered how the female half of the father/daughter duo, Libby Robinson, managed it in killer heels. I had a nightmare flashback to my Grade 5 piano exam, when uncontrollably shaking legs meant that any attempt at pedal control was a write-off. Maybe six-inch stilettos would have helped.

The reminiscences didn't stop there, thank goodness, because the evening brought back happy memories of learning and performing the piece, particularly the seemingly thousands of Amens that taxed us in frantic fugue fashion. One such Amen-littered movement was *Cum Sancto Spiritu,* my favourite, so I enjoyed mentally singing along to that one, although its closing section took me by surprise as it defined the term *prestissimo.* Or maybe more accurately *più presto possibile.* Had the conductor suddenly remembered he'd left the washing on the line too? I also couldn't help noticing the open 'a' sound in the oft-repeated 'sancto', remembering the rather classier 'ah' version we were exhorted to come out with. But let's not go in for choir wars, it was a lovely performance. Even if it wasn't as good as ours.

Even someone who claims that a music theory exam can be made to sound interesting would be pushing her luck in trying to introduce a wow factor to a description of an EGM. However, said meeting played a significant role in how this year of living musically would pan out – or indeed, whether it would be curtailed to nine months – so, dear reader, it's unavoidable.

In order to silence any potential critics, I'd prepared an introductory speech outlining the sequence of events that had brought us to the point of needing a vote. Not wanting to waste time before our scheduled rehearsal, everyone listened politely and applauded 'the workers' when I asked them to. There were a few comments and questions from the usual suspects, but nothing I couldn't handle. Then followed a quick shuffling of ballot papers, and before we knew it, it was all over. While the Treasurer and Secretary went behind the scenes to count the votes, I tried to concentrate on our next instalment of note-bashing through John Rutter's *Birthday Madrigals*. Would we end up singing 'Come live with me …' to The Other Choir? This seemed unlikely, given the many advance proxy votes I'd received in favour of the status quo, but as some wise if politically-incorrect person once said: 'It ain't over till the fat lady sings.'

I needn't have worried, as the consensus was a rather convincing 'no' to the merger, and nobody seemed shocked or outraged when it was announced in the interval. Along with my EGM speech, I'd also prepared two tactful responses to The Other Choir, one for each eventuality, and I emailed my counterpart the correct one as soon as I got home. Job done. As soon as I pressed 'send', in came another message from him, which must have crossed with mine, asking for the outcome. 'Oh good,' I thought, 'looks like he'll read it straight away.' So I was rather surprised by a phone call first thing in the morning: 'What was the result of your EGM?' I could hardly say 'I'm not telling you; read my painstakingly prepared email!' so we briefly discussed the situation. Rather than sounding surprised or disappointed, The Other Chairman actually intimated that they'd reached a similar conclusion about the difficulties of working with an enlarged choir. I put the phone down, thinking 'Good job we had a trial run then, wasn't it?' but expected some further comment following The Other Choir's committee meeting that evening. The silence, one might say, was deafening.

May
Shaping our destiny

We'd purposely called the EGM for the earliest feasible date in the summer term so that everyone concerned would then be free to make forward plans as appropriate. Regardless of the outcome, though, this term was always destined to be a single choir affair, as amalgamation – should it happen – wouldn't take place overnight.

On top of that, we always found numbers dwindled in the summer, as many members found they were less able to commit to Monday evening rehearsals due to holidays or other seasonal pursuits. As for me, I miss it enough during the school holiday shut-down; I doubt I'd survive a whole term away from it. The singing, that is, not the hassle.

So we were rather a select bunch of around 60 for our planned repertoire. I use 'planned' in a slightly loose sense, as another idiosyncrasy of the summer term – an opportunity to lighten up a little after the traditional classical fare of the autumn and spring – tended to have something of a 'make it up as you go along' feel.

John Rutter's *Birthday Madrigals* were definitely on the programme – the whole suite of five as opposed to the abridged version we'd tackled the year before – and through the MD's connections we were lucky enough to look forward to the composer himself coming to lead a rehearsal nearer the performance deadline. A buzz of awed excitement rose from the choir when this was announced, and we happily traipsed into split rehearsals for a few weeks to note-bash our way through the tricky jazz rhythms and close harmonies of our *cuckoos, oo-oos* and *doo-ba-doos.* The idea was that, just as the CM apparently blitzes her house in readiness for the arrival of her cleaner, we should be as prepared as possible for the maestro's visit.

Fair enough, as long as it wasn't to the detriment of another hour and a half's worth of performance that would need preparing.

Round about now I began to experience pain in my thumb. Not the one I'd fallen on so unceremoniously while stage-building, but my right one. Could it have been a delayed reaction to the jolt, as I was after all holding a chair aloft when I took the tumble? Only when some part of the body starts to go wrong do we realise how useful it is. I began to appreciate just what demands I place on this humble digit and became acutely aware of the specific grips employed in opening jars, turning on taps, manipulating a mouse (the computer component, not the rodent) when dealing with office spreadsheets – one of my least favourite occupations in 'real life' but one which realistically I wouldn't suddenly be allowed to relinquish. All of these had me wincing, but worse still it put the arghh! into arpeggio. I knew that pieces had been written for one-handed pianists, but as a compromise I wondered whether anything was available specifically for those squeamish about tucking their right thumb under the other fingers. Not only was it my right thumb, it was also my write thumb. Had I irreparably damaged it through my preferred method of pouring thoughts onto paper via a presumably-too-tightly-gripped pencil, its satisfyingly scratchy sound a catalyst to the creative process? Would I have to grasp the nettle – not too firmly, of course – and adopt the 21st century habit of composing directly onto the computer, albeit with the minimum of mouse-massaging?

The doctor sent me for an x-ray, just in case there was a fracture, and during the week's wait for the results I stayed away from the piano altogether, fearing the possibility of inflicting more damage. It began to feel a bit better, which was bittersweet because after my late encounter with the instrument I didn't wanted it to be quite so brief. Note to potential radio serialisers: Rachmaninov's 2nd Piano Concerto as the background music could usefully accompany this chapter. Apart from the bit that's coming up, which for reasons that will become apparent needs a violin soundtrack.

The x-ray revealed no fracture, but some degenerative changes to the interphalangeal and carpometacarpal joints. In layman's terms, I think this meant general wear and tear, presumably part of the ageing process. I was reassured to be told it wouldn't necessarily get worse, and started making strategies to cope with it. My pencils were adorned with blobby accoutrements which relaxed my grip, and as long as I didn't overdo the multi-octave arpeggios, some gentle piano playing was bearable. Anybody overhearing me might have a different opinion, of course, but at least it didn't hurt. Hopefully the physiotherapist, to whom I was to be referred, would conclude that playing was a help more than a hindrance. There's nothing like the threat of something being taken away from you for a sudden redoubling of interest. Or as Joni Mitchell once sang: *you don't know what you've got 'til it's gone.*

When I booked tickets for a coffee morning featuring conversation with Tasmin Little, I didn't expect to hear that her coffee-making skills allegedly rivalled her fiddle-playing. That would certainly be well worth tasting, and something to add to my repertoire of music-related ambitions. Not that Tasmin provided the coffee at the event at the Spring Sounds Festival in Stratford-upon-Avon, nor did she even drink any. Instead, as she took her seat in front of a score of people in the elegant surroundings of the riverside hotel, she asked for a glass of water.

'Tap water will do, or anything without bubbles.'

'Yes, Tasmin only drinks bubbles after concerts,' teased David Curtis, who the previous evening had conducted Tasmin and the Orchestra of the Swan in the Festival's opening performance. Tasmin appeared mock shocked at this revelation, then everyone visibly relaxed as she let rip with her infectious laugh. Much of the unashamedly bubbly repartee between them during the coffee morning related back to the concert, as they grappled with the question 'What does it take to be a maestro?'

A first-time OOTS concert-goer, I'd come down specially for the Festival, bringing my mother for a surprise birthday treat. No coincidence, then, that the programme included Haydn's (yes, him again) *Surprise Symphony*, so called because of the sudden dramatically loud chord played after a very quiet, tranquil theme, apparently added by the composer as a dynamic reminder to his audiences to pay attention throughout the whole piece. I couldn't help wondering what Haydn would have made of the elderly gentleman next door but one to me, blissfully dozing throughout the whole sparkling conversation between David and Tasmin.

The intimate, informal setting of the coffee morning echoed that of the performance at the Civic Hall. The modern interior of the Hall struck quite a contrast with the Georgian exterior. It was modest in size, with a wooden cone-like roof that cast a warm glow over the orchestra. They played at ground level surrounded by chairs on three sides, for all the world like a Shakespearean apron stage.

There was an immediate connection between players and audience, due in some measure to David's words of welcome. His excitement was palpable, and even when he turned round to face his orchestra, you could tell he was still smiling. Actually, you could hear it in their playing. In deference to the location, the Bard got a significant look-in with the opening number, the Scherzo and Nocturne from Mendelssohn's *A Midsummer Night's Dream*, its fairytale atmosphere evoked by lovely warm strings.

Then followed a marked seasonal change, with the world première of Roxanna Panufnik's *Tibetan Winter*, part of a 21st Century Four Seasons, specially commissioned for Spring Sounds. The programme notes indicated it would last approximately five minutes, perhaps to reassure audience members who were a little wary of new music. Personally, I could have listened to it all over again, and I certainly wasn't alone. It was composed for strings, with Tasmin and her 1757 Guadagnini violin in the leading role. However, the piece began, after an initial expectant hush, by the appropriately-named multi-tasking cellist, Nick Stringfellow, striking a Tibetan 'singing bowl'. As the reverberations echoed upwards, so an intensifying of that meditative hush seemed to penetrate deep into the Hall. Clearly the silences – beautifully timed – were an integral part of what the music had to say, emphasising the remote chill of the shivering, trembling strings. I tried in vain to identify how the intervals and rhythms worked together to produce that distinctive oriental sound, and instead settled for simply being transported.

After a further respectful hush, the warmth instantly returned in the shape of the audience's enthusiastic reception and an emotional embrace between composer and exponent. At the coffee morning, when David and Tasmin emphasised the crucial role of the audience in live performance, I asked Tasmin how it felt to play in the presence of the composer. She explained how they'd liaised during the piece's composition, working through a series of 'wish lists'. This would rarely be face to face, though, and Tasmin described how she found herself playing certain passages – to iron out how best to play the grace notes, for example – down the telephone to Roxanna. While everyone else chuckled at the bizarre picture this conjured up, I whispered to my Mum that this would make a welcome alternative to the usual call-centre queue 'music'.

But that, of course, is a world away from live performance, with the interaction of everyone in the room. Nobody at the coffee morning disagreed with David's appreciation of Tasmin's playing *with* the orchestra, in the sense of being truly involved with them as opposed to simply playing in front of them. True teamwork. Body language, eye contact, evident listening and mutual enjoyment all played a dramatic and valuable part, both in *Tibetan Winter* and Mendelssohn's *Violin Concerto,* which rounded off the concert with a flourish. Further crucial elements of live performance are the audience and their reaction – the musicians agreeing that picking up the atmosphere from a good crowd can take your performance a notch higher – and the fact that by definition each occasion is a unique, never-to-be-repeated experience. Even when performing exactly the same programme in exactly the same venue. It may be dependent on what you had for dinner, or how well you slept the night before. Each time it will vary in its own blend of inspiration, challenge, reward and that indefinable something that we'll have to call magic.

Particularly unique was the privilege of hearing a piece played in public for the very first time. Not only that, we were also treated to the UK première of American composer Frank James Staneck's *A Suite for Ursula,* a tribute to the wife of Ralph Vaughan Williams. After my rather recent immersion in RVW's music, I enjoyed picking out the evident influences in Staneck's work. The folksy, modal harmonies and changing time-signatures (at least that's how I heard them, though I didn't see the score) lent the three movements a bouncy, skip-along quality with a modern twist. Very easy on the ear, and again very much appreciated by the audience, amongst whom sat the beaming composer himself.

At every step, the multi-faceted teamwork aspect of music-making was underlined, although Tasmin almost dispelled this when, with a twinkle in her eye, she asserted that 'You have to trust your own judgment, no matter what the conductor says!' David's turn for mock shock. Tasmin has begun to take her own place on the conductor's podium, though – 'not part of my life plan,' she confessed – receiving reviews in Seattle such as 'Where has Tasmin Little been all my life?' She and David passed the baton to and fro in a lively discussion about how to get the best from an orchestra, based on a starting point assumption that the whole team has the same ultimate goal and that it's an inclusive process. Tasmin drew on her experience of a raft of famous names and their distinctive techniques: 'Comrades, wouldn't it be wonderful if the horns came in a bit earlier there?' being gentler than 'Horns, you're late!' and of first and second violins being slightly out of sync, 'If you don't play together, I don't know where to put the beat!'

David agreed that the musicians' ability to listen to each other, as though in a chamber ensemble, made the conductor's job a whole lot easier, and as long as there's a strong multi-way trust between orchestra, conductor and soloist, the act of conducting can be kept very spare. He recalled a conducting course he'd been on, where he'd taken copious notes, which he'd eventually condensed into: Slower, deeper, less … learn the bloody score!

He also likened the score to an Ordnance Survey map. 'It's all very well planning it out on a flat piece of paper, where all the symbols represent some landmark or undulation, but it's only when you actually take the journey that the lie of the land unfolds before and around you.' Similarly, bringing music to life is a constantly creative process, whether from the perspective of composer, conductor, performer or audience.

Someone asked about the variation in audience attitudes in Tasmin's worldwide touring venues. She pinpointed the subtle difference between the extreme quietness of the Japanese and polite reserve of the British, commenting that in fact silence and contemplation can play a very important role in certain circumstances – again referring in particular to Roxanna's new piece. At the opposite extreme came Italian passion and American volubility. Whatever her audience, Tasmin would always follow her actor father's advice with regard to presentation. Her performance would begin with the audience's first glimpse of the tip of her nose and finish with the final flourish of her retreating skirt. Sound advice for a world-class soloist, certainly, but as performance discipline goes, maybe worth bearing in mind even by an amateur provincial choir.

With The Vote out of the way, the choir was once more in a position to shape its own destiny, even if it was sensibly acknowledged that we should maintain open channels of communication with other local choirs. But when the XC suggested that a variation of the Go Betweens be kept on, to facilitate inter-choir liaison and avoid clashes in programming, dates and venues, I was utterly dismayed. Hiding behind the smokescreen of the VC's pre-existing attempts to get such a system operational, I managed to avoid saying outright that I'd like to be allowed to get on with it now, please.

And there was plenty to get on with, namely programming the following year, to include the all-but-certain visit of our French exchange choir. Deciding on what music to tackle would, under normal circumstances, have been done and dusted long before this, but our circumstances had hardly been normal. Until we knew whether we'd continue as a choir of 100 or expand to 150, with the possible constraints imposed by local council affiliation, our future menu had had to remain a movable feast.

Even with the kitchen to ourselves again, it wasn't a case of meekly saying 'Yes, chef!' when the MD announced the juicy morsels he had in store for 100 hungry mouths. The recent round of deliberations seemed to have given the Committee an appetite for re-assessing our *raison d'être* (might as well get into French mode sooner rather than later) and were clamouring for the choir to be given more opportunity to sing. Sounds obvious, you might say, but in certain choral works there's strangely little choral singing, with great chunks of solo work in between. 'Our audiences come to hear us, accompanied by orchestra and soloists, not the other way round,' was becoming a familiar theme. Herein lay the dilemma, though, given a finite amount of time for rehearsals: if works were chosen with more choral content, unless they were dead easy they'd either take longer to learn or the style and polish would have to give. A third alternative was to motivate everyone to commit to private practice between rehearsal, but this was the real world, after all. Could I persuade the MD to discuss this fine balancing act between quality and quantity?

Yes, taking advantage of a post-rehearsal swift half at the Mermaid, with the purpose of gleaning the MD's proposed programme for the following year, I asked how he thought we were progressing with learning our current repertoire. He was in his element tackling the tricky harmonies of Vaughan Williams' *Full Fathom Five*, and seemed genuinely surprised when, summoning up as much tact as I could, I suggested it might be just a little ambitious. Dividing the sopranos into four separate parts might not have been quite so bad if Shakespeare's words had been a little more inspiring. Sorry, Shakespeare, but repeating *Ding ... ding ... ding ...* many times over, followed by the somewhat more interesting, if unfathomable, *Nothing of him that doth fade, But doth suffer a sea change Into something rich and strange* (accompanied by a strange harmony indeed), and concluding with a peal of a couple of pages' worth of *ding dong bell* over and over again, just felt like a death knell. Allegedly, when successful it could be beautifully atmospheric, but in reality I had my doubts whether we were up to it. Wouldn't we be better off devoting our energies to something more attainable and that everyone would enjoy learning? The MD assured me that it was just experimental at this stage, and he'd reserve judgment on its inclusion in our programme until we'd had a concerted effort at it the following week. When all the bells had dinged their final dong, after all, it would only fill a few minutes' performance time anyway. Not unlike an author labouring over each highly crafted word, only for her reader to whip through the page in a matter of seconds.

An antidote to all this large-scale choral mayhem came in the shape of Lyra, a fine vocal ensemble from St Petersburg visiting our local church, appropriately St Peter's. 'Now we present for you some songs from Rachmaninov's *Vespers*,' declared Andrey. 'Normally they are sung back home in Russia by huge choirs, but,' he said, smiling at his three companions and then at the audience, 'you'll have to pretend!' And the four voices joined in *Bogoroditsye Dyevo*, familiar to me as *Hail, O*

Virgin Mother but altogether more moving in the mother tongue. A gradual crescendo finally filled the sandstone space with electrifying emotional intensity, followed by a sudden calm once more. I was certain this one would feature in my weekend course in the Cotswolds next month, and I couldn't wait.

They were young but accomplished singers, displaying a mixture of poise and humility that particularly suited the liturgical pieces of the first half. Largely unaccompanied, as would be expected of Russian church music, the songs began with Andrey checking the pitch with his tuning fork and humming their starting notes. From the depth of the bass voice to the soaring soprano, they were beautifully blended. The audience may not have understood the words, but the singers somehow got their stories across anyway, proving once again the universality of music. I was in awe of their breath control and the big voices projected from their slim bodies, not to mention their versatility. As well as the ensemble pieces, they each performed solos, and where these were from the European repertoire they took turns to accompany each other on the piano.

For the second half there was a costume change, and tux and concert frock were replaced by national dress in scarlet with gold motifs, tassels and stylised flowers. It was the turn of Russian folk music. We didn't quite get Cossack dancing, but the theatricality and playfulness put big smiles on everyone's faces, and the visitors began to seem like old friends. No inhibitions, then, for the last official number, which demanded audience participation; it was the well-known *Kalinka,* with its haunting rhythms and exciting quickening tempo, accompanied by hand-clapping and more than a little laughter. Lyra took the enthusiastic applause in traditional Russian fashion, placing right hand on left shoulder and bowing deeply. There was something rather humble about the gesture, especially given the quality of the evening's entertainment, then Andrey broke the spell: 'OK, if you insist, we'll give you an encore!' Which turned out to be a traditional toast, brief but full of fun, which sent everyone home literally on a high note.

High notes, it seemed, were all I'd be getting at my weekend singing holiday, as the news emerged that not enough men had been recruited and the programme was to be re-jigged to accommodate female voices only. It would still be Russian and Eastern European music, which was difficult to imagine without the richness of those bass notes, but singing just with ladies would make an interesting concept in its own right, so I hoped for the best. It's a perennial problem, though, and it would be good to tempt more men into the wonderful world of choral singing, if this volume ever appeals to anyone apart from the author and her agent. And if it ever gets finished, for that matter.

Here's a conundrum for a novice writer: what do you do when, nine months into a year-long memoir, it all becomes too painful to write about? Literary labour pains, perhaps. Abort the whole thing and turn to fiction instead, based on the premise that you can make your characters do what you want? There again, maybe not, as the experts would surely warn that your creations have a tendency to take on a life-force of their own if you're doing it right. Or perhaps pour it all out anyway, a kind of therapeutic drivel that you realise will have to be thoroughly sanitised before going anywhere near a publisher. If not shredded. The tutors always spoke about finding your 'voice' – certainly an interesting dimension for someone keen to write about singing – something altogether more personal than mere style. Perhaps an uninhibited unburdening of soul onto paper would bring me closer to that than ever before. Without the camouflage of humour, as my capacity for finding the funny side at this point wore so thin as to dwindle almost to *niente*, just like those damned bells at the end of *Full Fathom Five.* Following on from a rehearsal in which we toiled over trying to perfect its notes and timing, first in a laborious sectional and then with marginal success in full choir mode, I wasn't in the best frame of mind for our scheduled Committee meeting. Mind you, if the MD was ambitious in his choice of music, the length of my agenda was even more so. The fine balance between getting the various tasks done and allowing time for discussion was proving difficult to manage, with a constant sense of rushing and being left with loose ends to tie up. That was par for the course, though. The worry this time was a feeling of dejection and an unaccustomed niggling inner voice that taunted 'why bother, if you're not enjoying it?' My actual voice came out with some heartfelt, though regrettable, comments about whether we'd ever be ready for performance at this rate, and maybe it would be better not to even have a concert, to which the response was that it's always worth working hard at something tricky because you get it right eventually. Depends when 'eventually' is, I suppose, and whether alongside it we could prepare sufficient other material to entertain our paying public.

Alongside all that, we also had future projects to plan for. If this year had been unusual (and it had) the following choir year would also offer significant extra challenges. Preparing for the French visitors would have us beavering away a year ahead to secure bookings for concert venues and peripheral social activities. 'Who'd like to take the lead on this one?' I asked hopefully. Several of my Committee colleagues put themselves forward to take care of specific aspects of the project, but no willing ringleader emerged at first. What's the French for 'muggins'? Thankfully, the XC, who had been the driving force behind the link in the first place, agreed to don his exchange-organising *chapeau*. And the VC had thoughtfully taken the lead in securing our contribution to the Churches Conservation Trust 'Birthday Song' celebrations in October, which meant we could advertise ourselves as one of 40 choirs nationwide selected to commemorate their 40th anniversary. This set in train yet another sub-committee's worth of preparations for a day's workshop to be led by the MD – no small feat of organisational, promotional and financial planning, the bottom line even being influenced by the hire of portaloos.

Meanwhile, though, the current term's work couldn't be neglected, and time was marching on in a *marziale* sort of way. The MD requested an extra rehearsal in place of the usual half-term break. Quite how wise it was to introduce several new pieces, at a time when substantial numbers were away in some sunny clime, is debatable, but for me it was a huge relief to be faced once again with music that I immediately knew I was going to enjoy. The appeal lay, I realised, as much with the meaningful words as with the beautiful lyrical music. Having said that, at first glance I mistook Campion's *Never weather-beaten sail* for a soggy mollusc. Optically-challenged as I clearly was, I could sympathise with the composer (he wrote the words too) as, on his metaphorical voyage towards death, he longed for *...Heav'n's high Paradise. Cold age deafs not there our ears, nor vapour dims our eyes ...* The odd C sharp snuck into the soprano line where it should have been a natural, but otherwise it was fairly straightforward and encouragingly achievable. I still think it sounded better with sharps, though. I think I tried a few adjustments to Pilkington's *Rest, sweet nymphs* too, in which the perfect

4th in bar 8 was less than perfect the way I sang it, but the main thing was that I felt compelled to pour some expression into the lullaby strains invoking golden sleep to charm their *star brighter eyes.* As for Finzi's *My spirit sang all day*, this one did exactly what it said on the tin. With lovely joyful words by Robert Bridges and plenty of scope for uplifting dynamics, I was more than happy to have it flitting around my brain – and spirit – between rehearsals. The rhythm might have been a bit fiddly, but not, according to the MD 'as difficult as you made it sound'. Just because I thought I'd once again found something I was going to be able to sing, this was no time for complacency, clearly.

But the important thing was that it was music itself that brought me back to a place of 'calm contentments' – another phrase borrowed from Pilkington's piece, written by that ubiquitous lyricist, Anon – at least for a time. Switching on the car stereo after a challenging day at the office always provided a merciful escape route, as well, but one evening I went one better and made my way to the Music Department's end-of-year show. At this point I could address all dictionary compilers: next time you're searching for inspiration for the definition of 'eclectic', look no further. This year's concert, at the same church where we'd sung *The Creation*, truly had something for everyone.

The overriding impression whenever I see these young musicians at work is of a great big family enjoying themselves and their music. And within that family, each has different talents to offer. The first half showcased the more traditional elements, with orchestral music from Rossini and Fauré, and classical choices from the Flute Choir – a wonderful vehicle for Handel's *Arrival of the Queen of Sheba,* taking me back to my musings about being fitted with castors – and Clarinet Choir too. But the flutes also ventured into unfamiliar territory with Pierre Paubon's atmospheric, haunting *Anouchka,* which appeared technically demanding and showed off their fine breath control. The clarinet ensemble also gave us a contrast, balancing their Mozart *Allegro* with Abreu's *Tico Tico,* the samba rhythms oozing Brazilian sunshine and setting the audience's feet tapping.

Half the audience couldn't see the solo violinist in the side balcony, but to be fair, even if she'd been within my field of vision, I'd have listened to the Bach *Sarabande* with closed eyes, so exquisite was her interpretation.

There was certainly an interesting use of the space in the church, especially bearing in mind our deliberations should we have needed to station some of our combined choir in the balcony. The audience swivelled and craned to see the university choir up there, alongside the organ that accompanied them. Benjamin Britten's *Rejoice in the Lamb* struck me as very ambitious, with its lack of easily graspable 'tune' and absolute mayhem of words, based on a poem written by Christopher Smart whilst in a lunatic asylum. However, the choir achieved it with some style, and the occasional nugget, portraying an overall sense of creation praising God in many and various ways. Written by a madman or not, surely nobody could fail to enjoy his appreciation of his cat: 'For God has blessed him in the variety of his movements. For there is nothing sweeter than his peace when at rest. For I am possessed of a cat, surpassing in beauty, from whom I take occasion to bless Almighty God.'

No sooner was the refreshment interval over than the Chamber Choir were extolling the virtues of coffee and tea in *Java Jive,* accompanied by a mellow blend of organ and clicking fingers, and setting the audience swaying. Again, I couldn't see the singers, but I could hear the smiles. A change of pace brought us Karl Jenkins' *Adiemus*, its African feel transporting us to the dusty plains, with a striking *crescendo* and the unexpected and effective addition of recorders.

Time to speed up again at the hands of a jazz pianist who rejoiced in the name of Harwood Shing. His draw-dropping command of Oscar Peterson's *Oscar's Boogaloo* brought to mind an unstoppable train, the audience nodding their heads as they were propelled along on the exciting journey. Make mine a return.

The resident rock band seemed a little incongruous within the hallowed walls, but nobody could fault the enthusiasm and exuberance, nor, of course, the appeal to the student age-group. Fronting the Jazz Orchestra, a young lady with a sparkly headband and velvet voice gave us a soulful *When Sunny Gets Blue*, and a tiny person with a voice and a half made *Big Spender* her own.

Secular to sacred once more, the Music Theatre Group re-introduced a note of gentle calm with *Day by Day*. The lead singer's clear, level voice was joined by some lovely sweet harmonies. The slow tempo gave way to an *accelerando* and as the music became more complex so did the whole performance, with the addition of extra layers, first swaying and then clapping, before coming full circle to a serene close.

The official closing number of the evening was *Bohemian Rhapsody*, and that would have been show-stopper enough. But in the context of saying farewell to the departing third years, there followed an encore, George Michael's *Faith*. If a whole university Music Department could get away with singing that to the accompaniment of a couple of ukuleles, then surely the students could have faith in themselves, whatever lay ahead.

There was something about this month, though, that threatened to knock the optimism out of me. I wasn't actively looking for difficulties, they just found me. With just three weeks' notice, a letter arrived announcing that my weekend singing course had been cancelled altogether. I imagined many of the ladies found they didn't like the sound of it any more, once it had been declared a female voices event, and had pulled out, leaving too few to make it viable. Did these people not realise the huge contribution this was supposed to make to my début writing masterpiece? Gallivanting around Google merely revealed several tasty treats that I'd just missed, or summer schools that would clash with our family holiday, so I spent the next day or so being unbearable. You could say my nearest and dearest were suffering for my art.

June
A composer calls

I suppose that if I'd recognised how important it was for me to include an account of my adventures on a residential weekend, I would have scheduled it earlier in my year of living musically, or made contingency plans. Would I ever find a comparable alternative that I could manage within the timeframe? As it turned out, I did find an alternative, but it wasn't exactly comparable and it remained to be seen whether I'd manage it. One thing's for certain: I wouldn't have had the nerve to book this one earlier in the year, and the fact that I did so now was an indication that, whatever else my chairmanship had done to me, it had given me confidence. Or bravado. Hopefully not ill-founded.

My wanderings around the web were frustratingly non-productive when searching under 'choral courses'. 'Try Jackdaws,' suggested the MD, 'they do weekends, and they're reputable.' As though in proof of this last statement, he added 'I've been there myself.' I hadn't come across that one, and when I found their website it became apparent why. No choral courses. Maybe time to think laterally. There were all manner of vocal and instrumental workshops, but it all looked a bit high-powered, the listings strewn with the dreaded phrase 'Grade 8' in the ability column. Although Jackdaws sounded idyllic, tucked away in rural Somerset, at first glance it was also tucked away out of my league.

Something called 'Pianos for All' was offered, though, which if anything I was overqualified for, giving people of humble abilities the chance to enjoy some ensemble work on the usually solitary instrument. Sounded fun. Unfortunately this was yet another that I'd just missed. Should I try my luck at a Piano Workshop in

September, pitched at Grade 5 and above? Certainly if I ever wished to tackle those exam nerves and attempt Grade 6, the experience of undergoing some intensive training in company with other people would pay dividends.

Another option brought me back to my more portable instrument. 'Discover your Voice' – a title of which my writing tutors would doubtless have approved – had an even less threatening ability level attached. Beginners. After ten years in the choir, I wouldn't be so falsely modest as to claim I couldn't sing, and yet this course offered the chance to learn some fundamental techniques, the sorts of things I'd only ever picked up instinctively. Could the tutor help me find fresh inspiration by teaching me how to breathe? More to the point, would I have the courage to sing solo, away from the usual safety in numbers, as this course would demand? In front of friends, forget it, but amongst complete strangers, possibly so. So I booked it, and looked forward to the end of the month. If nothing else, it should prove to be something different to write home about. Hopefully it wouldn't risk turning the memoir into a farce or a tragedy.

Meanwhile, a summer event was approaching that had become one of the choir's annual fundraising extravaganzas. The XC and his wife kindly opened up their beautiful garden for an afternoon of relaxation, conversation and consumption of vast amounts of tea and cake. The ordered sunny weather turned up bang on cue, as did the Red Arrows, courtesy of the local RAF air show. The resulting profits were more than welcome in the kitty that was accumulating for hospitality for the French choir's visit. Offering thanks for the success of the occasion, I encouraged other members to come up with their own fundraising initiatives. 'Calendar Girls?'

suggested the MD, eyebrows raised and trying to look as innocent as the boy treble he once was. With an alacrity that surprised even myself, I countered with 'Calendar Boys?' To preserve modesty, we'd have to have strategically-placed musical notes, although in some instances we'd need considerably larger crotchets. It then occurred to me that there could be some handy spin-offs. No more need we debate concert dress, and unrest about the choir's name could be silenced forever by assuming the highly marketable title The Naked Choir. Quite where the MD would put his tuning fork, though, is anybody's guess.

By the time John Rutter's visit to the choir came around, it seemed like we'd worked so hard on the music that there'd be little more to learn. Not that we'd overdone it, and I certainly wasn't in danger of getting fed up of the *Birthday Madrigals*. On the contrary, now that we knew them pretty well, they were a real pleasure to sing, with a swing, and in fact I couldn't imagine it was possible to be more smitten with them. Add the composer himself into the mix, though, and the experience took on a whole extra dimension.

I wasn't sure of the protocols for offering hospitality to world-class composers, but I was thrilled when John accepted my invitation to a pre-rehearsal dinner at our second home, the Mermaid. Much as it would have been wonderful to keep him all to myself, a fit of public-spiritedness got the better of me and I invited the committee too, although most said they'd just join us afterwards for coffee. A rather dull day had turned into a beautiful summer's evening and I hugged my glass of sparkling water as I waited for the great man to arrive. Once welcomes and introductions had been seen to, I offered to order a drink while he chose from the menu. 'Just a sparkling water, please.' This was looking better and better. He didn't order the same food as me, but I was inordinately pleased that we shared the same taste in beverages. Completely irrationally, it reinforced my aspirations as a 'creative'.

The MD himself arrived long-distance from a day at the examining front, with just enough time to avoid indigestion. I'd promised him a Mermaid takeaway if he was late – 'a bit chewy, perhaps, but musicians like scales, don't they?' Others made their entries at varying times for coffee, such that the whole occasion resembled a complicated choral work with little compositional discipline, and yet the atmosphere was relaxed and more leisurely than I'd feared, given the tight timescales. There was plenty of laughter. I sat there like a Cheshire Cat, relishing the special occasion.

I did manage some sparkling conversation, to match John's drink and mine, you see. He'd come all the way up from Cambridge to join us, and I asked about his other travels. 'Last week I was in Cologne,' he said, 'leading workshops for a few thousand people over a few days. Marvellous. Then on Thursday I'm off to New York, to do my *Requiem* and Mozart's' – it was wonderful how that tripped off the tongue, almost like having Wolfgang at the table with us as well – 'at Carnegie Hall, with singers handpicked from choirs all over the States.' What on earth was this man going to make of our efforts, I couldn't help wondering? But despite his high-powered and high profile schedule, his feet seemed truly on the ground. Revealing an unexpected vulnerability, he wondered what it was going to be like to lead The Big Sing for the first time, when the Royal Albert Hall would be filled with amateurs. Nothing short of brilliant, I imagined, but he seemed genuinely to wonder whether he could handle it! Had it not coincided with our own concert weekend, I would have been down there, but instead I marvelled again at our good fortune in having this more personal arrangement.

More personal still, of course, is spending time alone, and John reflected on that solitary side of his life, composing. There wasn't time to dig deeper, but I sensed an almost-reluctance, that perhaps he doesn't care so much for being in isolation and yet at the same time it's a compulsion.

Like writing.

One of our altos confided in me that she was like a dizzy schoolgirl in anticipation of our VIP visitor. So when John exhorted greater attack at the opening of *It was a lover and his lass* – 'I like my altos fiery!' – I feared for a fainting fit. The atmosphere from the first note, though displaying unprecedented best behaviour from our members, was thoroughly relaxed. Considering he'd never worked with us before, the maestro had the measure of us straight away. During the hour or so that sped by, he managed the dual achievement of reassuring us that we were in with a chance of pulling off a reasonable performance and pinpointing areas where we could add more polish. And he made us want to shine.

I had an inkling we'd be in for some musical gems, of course, but what took me by surprise was the wicked sense of humour. This came out in the composer's evident relish for the language and meaning within the texts, full of the innuendo and double-entendre typical of the era. Metaphorical light bulbs pinged on around me as some of my colleagues, listening to John's emphasis and explanation, realised for the first time just what Shakespeare, Marlowe and Raleigh were going on about. In *Come live with me* John urged us to focus on the dialogue, which conveyed a story in this 'words-driven' movement. With intense concentration in his eyes, and metronomically clicking fingers, he helped us get into character – namely the gents were shepherds making multifarious promises but doubtless after one thing only, and the ladies seeing right through it and likely to have none of it ... although there was no harm in leading them on a bit. Offering a spot of 'retail therapy', the men sang *A gown made of the finest wool, Which from our pretty lambs we pull; Fair lin-èd slippers for the cold, with buckles of the purest gold'*, answered cynically by the ladies, *Thy gowns, thy shoes, thy beds of roses, Thy cap, thy kirtle, and thy posies Soon break, soon wither, soon forgotten, In folly ripe, in reason rotten.* All the ladies sang the last phrase in unison, right in the basement of the sopranos' range, hovering around and below middle C. The MD had encouraged us to adopt a chesty tone and shout it out with vehemence. John's reaction? A genuinely impressed 'Not bad!'

When daisies pied called for even greater bawdiness, but before John graphically illustrated how he wanted this story of bucolic adultery told – 'camp it up, gasp with lust!' – he highlighted the importance of correct balance between voices. The sopranos, with the tune, weren't to be drowned out by everyone else's fa-la-la'ing underneath. It was a question of realising whether at any given time you were the icing or the cake.

To carry his analogy a stage further, I can honestly say that John Rutter's rehearsal gave us not only the cake and the icing, but a generous helping of cherries and birthday candles on top. Surely it would light up our performance, give sustenance to our audience, and the overall winner would be the music, just as it should be.

Being totally engrossed in my world of what I like to call 'proper music', it came as a nasty shock to me, a couple of days before my trip to Jackdaws in Somerset, to learn that the Glastonbury Festival was taking place at the same time. And even I knew that was in Somerset, too. So rather than risking motorway jams,

I let the train take the strain. This had the extra advantage of letting me catch up on scribbling for posterity the musical experiences that were coming thick and fast. Not that the writing got too much attention on the return journey, as by the end of the weekend I was totally shattered. But in a good way. And an unexpected way. Let's say I discovered more than my voice.

After a trouble-free train journey, a taxi took me from Frome to my final destination. I thought I was in for a history lesson as the driver meandered his way down the tortuous narrow lane, Jackdaws nestling in the valley. 'It's like being back in Oliver Cromwell's time', he said, but that was as far as it went. He was simply referring to the unspoilt landscape and huddle of honey-coloured cottages.

Jackdaws itself was perfectly in keeping with this otherworldly atmosphere, and hidden from the country road by luxuriant vegetation. It could have been just another private residence, were it not for the plaque, declaring that it was opened as a music education trust by its Patron, Dame Joan Sutherland, in 1993. Long before the human singing began, birdsong could be heard in old English trees that rustled in the gentle breeze. There was virtually no other sound at all, apart from the occasional horse clopping across the stone bridge over the stream. I wasn't sure what was more welcome, the near-silence or the fresh, clear air.

'I think I'll cope with this', I thought, as I let myself in through the half-open wooden door. The illusion of wandering into one of the locals' cottages continued as I found myself not at a reception desk, nor were there any other trappings of commerce. Instead I was faced with a farmhouse kitchen, dominated just inside the front door by a large table invitingly set for a small crowd. I realised I was getting hungry when the smell of something spicy greeted my nostrils. 'Hello,

137

I'm Rosemarie', said an apron-clad lady wielding a wooden spoon. 'You're the first, but supper won't be long. Why don't you go and get acquainted with the house, and the others'll be here soon.' As indicated, I climbed the stairs, just to the side of a promising drinks trolley. The half-landing gave visitors a choice: left up another couple of steps to the large room that would be the scene of our musical endeavours over the next forty eight hours, or right into a small library. Actually the library spilled out onto the landing as well, with stacks of music dictionaries and labelled boxes. Inside was stuffed with well-used copies of just about every brand of vocal and instrumental music imaginable, the edges of the shelves proclaiming 'Oratorio by voice' or 'String quartets by composer A-Z' in careful script on bright yellow labels. Shelf-space had proved inadequate, though, and there were also piles on the floor and tables, and on a mini harpsichord hiding under a tapestry cloth. Underneath a baby grand piano there was a jumbled box of percussion instruments.

Despite all this potential for sound, everywhere was eerily quiet, until my fellow voice-discoverers arrived. Then a little bell rang summoning us to supper. It soon became apparent that although we might discover our voices, there was a strong possibility we'd lose our waistlines, as this was just the start of an onslaught of feeding over the course of the weekend. Over a scrummy soup that had us all guessing at the magic extra ingredients – butternut squash? coriander? – we introduced ourselves and discussed what we thought the weekend would bring.

The group was just a comfortable size, six delegates, tutor and accompanist. Nobody seemed wary of mucking in with strangers and we were quickly united in common purpose: discovering our voices – and, less predictably, helping each other discover theirs – and having a good time.

That lovely first supper was a great way to kick off the proceedings in relaxed style, but the formal introductions began upstairs afterwards, at our first session. We invaded a large room, dominated at one end by a magnificent Steinway. It stood in front of French windows giving onto a roof terrace, beyond which Jackdaws' gardens cocooned us from the outside world. Stylish pastel drawings lined the walls, each apparently depicting the same pair of twin girls playing music. Versatile twins, clearly, as their choice of matching instrument varied from picture to picture, along with the colour scheme. Otherwise, there were few distractions, just the practical paraphernalia needed by those intent on making music: a stash of music stands, and a full-length mirror, about which more below.

Before we even uttered a single musical note, our tutor Penny asked us to stand up in turn and say something of our background, experience and expectations. If I'd had any qualms about classing myself a beginner, this is where I realised I needn't have, as each of us had already made several strides, in varying directions, along that road of discovery. Hazel went first. She lived locally, had done the same course last year and enjoyed it so much that she'd come back for more. She was a sprightly 78 year-old who, in her succession of floral frocks, had the gentle mannerisms of an Edwardian lady. She sang with the village ladies' choir, who learned all their stuff by rote and performed without scores. Bliss! In my mind's eye, twenty-five Hazel-clones unswervingly watched their choir mistress. Those pictures of twins had a lot to answer for.

Next came Joy, who not only had been taking singing lessons but exams too. 'Beginners' had obviously been interpreted somewhat loosely. She led singing in church sometimes, and was looking for more confidence. Kate sang in various groups including an *a capella* choir, so must know a thing or two already. Anita, one of the most beautiful people I've ever met, both in the looks and personality departments, had years ago sung on the West End stage and was looking to regain some of the old confidence. This 'Beginners' lark was really taking a battering by now.

Graham, the only gentleman on the course apart from accompanist Tim, was closest in experience to myself, having sung for many years in a large choral society. He was also keen on amateur dramatics, and before the weekend was out this would become apparent in his choice of operatic aria.

Nobody seemed a shrinking violet, but when it was Anita's turn she asked 'Can't I stay sat down?' 'No!' was Penny's reaction, 'everyone has to practise being comfortable in a vulnerable position, which is exactly where you'll be when you sing on your own.' I suspect the delivery of our little speeches also gave her several clues about bad habits to be squashed, and, hopefully, strengths to be encouraged.

First things first, were we breathing properly? The act of singing took on a more physical dimension as Penny spoke of nourishing, feeding breath into the sound through a column of air. Shoulders shouldn't rise as we breathed in, instead the lungs must expand outwards. This involved a touchy-feely five minutes while, conga-fashion, we tested whether the required action was taking place in each other's ribcage. Pulled-in tummies were outlawed. There must be no obstructions in 'our instrument', so we needed to learn how to stand correctly with almost-bent knees, as though 'about to sit on a bar stool, with your bum tucked under and hands by your sides.' There was an awful lot to think about even before opening your mouth, but at last it was time for some music, or a warm-up at least. Every aspect of our vocal muscles was given a thorough work-out as we traipsed through scales and arpeggios, uttering an array of vowel sounds and consolidating our consonants.

'Who'd like to go first?' asked Penny, who unfortunately was labouring under the misapprehension that we'd all prepared something to sing. Evidently a crucial sentence had been omitted from the joining instructions. But a few had brought along their favourites and took to the floor. Hazel's sweet innocence, singing from the soul, struck a contrast with what Penny advocated for Anita. Diagnosed as singing a little sharp, she was encouraged to swivel her hips throughout the performance, to free up her diaphragm. Regardless of whether this produced a truer sound or not, it certainly made Graham's weekend.

The following morning was launched with an outdoor warm-up, standing in a circle on the lawn, amongst the willow sculptures. Not so much a warm-up, actually, more a meditation. It might have seemed a bit New Age, but it was so peaceful in the early morning sunshine that it worked, setting us up for another glorious day's music-making. The indoor warm-up was an operatic affair, in which we had to sing 'Bella Signora' up and down an arpeggio at the top of our voices, while simultaneously parading around the room gesticulating to our companions. A further loosening of the inhibitions, allegedly, as well as the muscular tensions. Those of us who hadn't yet sung took our turn and were coached in techniques to suit our particular foibles. The mirror came into play when Penny wanted us to see as well as hear the effects upon ourselves. She worked on the correct shapes required for formation of vowels and diphthongs. She had us holding flattened hands across our faces 'RAF-moustache-style' to feel the resonance in our cheekbones. She had us raising our eyebrows to look more animated, and threatened to stick sellotape on our foreheads if we frowned. Every now and then she plundered a box of tricks for an unlikely practice tool. A cork wedged between Kate's teeth forced her to overcome a tendency to sing through an almost-shut mouth. A feather boa jazzed up Anita's song, for the sake of relaxing her facial tensions.

When I surmised that my debut attempts at singing solo might turn out to be the stuff of tragedy or farce, I should perhaps have expected tears of either sadness or laughter. What I hadn't bargained for was weeping with raw emotion. As we went back inside Jackdaws after a coffee break in the sun, with only me left to take to the floor, I felt it was a case of 'last, and probably least'. Beginners' course or not, there were some hard acts to follow. I didn't feel consciously nervous though, because the atmosphere was so supportive and non-judgmental. The main difficulty was choosing what to sing as I hadn't prepared anything and was only familiar with choral material. There were scores of scores in which to find something suitable, and Mozart's *Ave Verum Corpus* seemed a good bet; it was quite some years since the choir had sung it, but it was a memorable and beautiful tune. It was one of the rare ones that we'd sung by heart, and the sort of music that spoke to the heart too, so I knew that coming from a starting point of the music communicating something to me, maybe I'd be in with a chance of communicating something with the music.

Trying to remain aware of the valuable lessons that Penny had taught about breathing, relaxation, facial positions and so on, I went for it, supported by Tim's versatility on the piano. Not from memory, which in all honesty I probably could have done, but with the safety net of a music stand between me and the rest of the class. Guess what? Nothing went horribly wrong. I ran out of breath here and there, realised I was holding my arms wrong, tensed my neck too much and didn't hold my head up enough. But I enjoyed it. I enjoyed the sound that came out. I even enjoyed people listening to the music, with me as the vehicle. Such lovely music. Then the work started. Penny's initial verdict was of a well-poised voice, which sounded rather complimentary, but she gauged that there was a whole lot more to come out. The main barrier was that I was too damn tense. 'Are you someone who likes to feel in control?' asked Penny, when I failed miserably to let my arms go suitably floppy. Perceptive lady. She tried leaning me against the wall for support. No good, still too tense. So it was 'Onto the floor, young lady, please!' I was made to feel the jute carpet supporting me. 'Melt into the floor, like milk.' Then I had to sing it all again, supine, to an open-mouthed 'ah' sound, while Penny manipulated my head from side to side to free up my neck muscles – I was forbidden from exercising any control over my own movements, apart from my breathing, lungs expanding downwards into the embrace of the floor. Amazing. I hadn't overcome it completely, as I was aware of my fingertips' grip against the fibrous surface, but my head seemed to have been exchanged with a ragdoll's. After another visible demonstration of correct breathing, involving a thick tome of Schubert songs being plonked on my midriff, I was allowed up again.

Back to the music stand to try it out with the newly-relaxed neck. Better, but room for improvement in the facial relaxation department, and scope for more resonance to come from the upper chest rather than throat. The latter was tackled by Penny's knuckles rapping continuously just below my collar bone to remind me to employ that particular area of my anatomy; the former by pulling forward my top lip between pinched forefinger and thumb. Despite this no doubt producing a totally bizarre spectacle to behold, the transforming effect on the sound was more than worth it. Soaring through the crescendo and shaping the dozen notes of the final 'in mortis', it was scarcely possible to believe the music was actually coming out of my mouth. Mine. Mozart, if you were listening, I hope you didn't mind that it reduced me to tears.

To break up the solo singing, and by way of light relief on what was quite an emotional journey, we learned a couple of pieces to sing together as rounds. *'How great is the pleasure, how sweet the delight/When friendship and music together unite;/ How great is the pleasure, how sweet the delight/When friends, in song, together unite;/Sweet, sweet, how sweet the delight/When harmony, sweet harmony and friendship unite.'* A suitable message to take back to the choir, I thought. I couldn't have put it better myself, so thank you, Mr Harrington. I did pen my own little poem, though: *Breathe deeply at peaceful Jackdaws/Relax and open your jaws;/Your voice you'll discover/O brave music lover;/Project, then collect your applause!* There was a solid sense of shared endeavour and mutual encouragement throughout the weekend – only a weekend; it felt like we'd known each other for ever! The listeners' eyes sparkled as we each made our solo offerings, identifying with our feelings and willing us to give of our best in the spotlight.

Graham's contribution cried out for footlights. He gave a spirited and comical performance as Papageno, the bird-catcher from *The Magic Flute,* complete with mock proposal to Hazel on bended knee. She turned him down, by the way. No matter that he forgot some of the words. Penny reckoned that was perfectly acceptable and admitted to occasionally extemporising on the professional stage, finding that the lyrics 'alpha romeo, spaghetti bolognese' made very convincing substitutes. Her only suggestion for improvement was to exploit Graham's evident theatrical bent, involving a trip through the French windows into the garden. The piano introduction started up again, and then Graham's bearded face appeared cautiously around the door, the shoulders below bedecked with fronds of leaves, his clothes and hair sprouting feathers here and there. I don't know how he kept his face straight.

We each had the chance to present three songs. Somewhat ambitiously, I opted next for *Pie Jesu* from Fauré's *Requiem;* I'd been one in a hundred singing the choral work, but was I out of my mind attempting the soprano solo? It's such a beautiful movement that I couldn't resist and as fortune favours the brave I finished up with a feeling of almost controlled powerfulness. Almost, except that Penny still had issues with the tension in my arms and while I was in mid-flow she pressed carrier bags full of music scores into my hands. Chairman becomes bag-lady. Then cleaning-lady: my rendition of *Amazing Grace* was applauded but Penny still wanted me to loosen up. I needed distracting. 'This piano's awfully dusty,' she said, proffering a silk scarf, 'see what you can do.' So while Tim played £37,000-worth of Steinway, I wandered around dusting it, bending and reaching across its vast expanse, simultaneously and almost incidentally singing *'How precious did that grace appear, The hour I first believed.'* It came up lovely. The piano that is, modesty forbids an opinion on my vocal performance.

Back to the communal singing, and things were shaping up nicely at choir, although you could occasionally hear the odd voice saying 'this doesn't sound very familiar – have we sung it before?' About ten days away from a concert, this wasn't the most encouraging comment ever, but we pressed on and hoped it would be 'alright on the night'. The greatest chunk of our energies had been devoted to madrigals, whether John Rutter's or the more traditional Elizabethan ones. The latter came from a large compendium, *Madrigals and Partsongs*, a choir-sized set of which we'd been lucky enough to acquire through receiving a local grant. *Opera Choruses* was another such volume, and over the years certain numbers had become fairly well-known territory for our lighter-themed summer concerts. Many's the time the XC displayed further talents during our renditions of the *Anvil Chorus* from Verdi's *Il trovatore,* earning him the unusual, perhaps even unique, accolade of Principal Anvilist. We could offer *The Chorus of the Hebrew Slaves* from Verdi's *Nabucco* in either English or Italian, although visitors from Venice or Verona might have found it all Greek. This one didn't need too much slave-driving on the part of the MD, but he had his work cut out steering us through a couple of new ones. Everybody recognises the *Bridal Chorus,* even if they don't realise it's from Wagner's *Lohengrin,* but since most brides make it down the aisle within a couple of dozen bars, and since she's more likely to be accompanied by organ than four-part choir, most of us found it quite a revelation tackling the whole piece as a choral work. Beautiful, but a bit difficult to handle, which I suppose could be said for some brides, too.

The most comforting thing that could be said about the *Waltz Scene* from Tchaikovsky's *Eugene Onegin* was that we didn't have to tackle it in Russian. If we pulled it off, this number would sit very nicely with the format of the evening's entertainment, as not only would we provide aural delights but gastronomic ones too at the post-performance social. We were meant to be peasants extolling the virtues of the food and wine on offer at a wonderful party, and after a flamboyant piano introduction we had to burst in, *forte,* with *'This is superb!'* Quite frankly, most times it really wasn't. Even if we got our first entry right, there was plenty of scope for making a shambles of the rest of them, the waltz rhythm playing tricks on the overlapping voices and doing its best to trip us up. Not to mention the notes. *'Such a surprise!'* we sopranos sang, the repeated As of the first three syllables followed by an F natural, then two and two-thirds bars later, the same phrase but with the final note going uphill to a B natural. Never failed to take me by surprise. Then there were the repeated sections, calling for manual as well as vocal dexterity, flicking back a few pages so we could once again tell everyone how splendid, delightful and well-planned everything was. And conversely, a whole chunk to be cut, the MD having taken a reality check on how much of it we'd be able to conquer. Because time was waltzing on.

July
Let nothing affright ye

And so our final evening rehearsal arrived. After the car-in-the-ditch incident and the lost-voice incident of the two previous terms, it was inevitable that some other obstacle lay in wait for the MD this time around. Coinciding with examining time again, this vital rehearsal presented him with a 7-hour round trip, as the Board in their wisdom had stationed him in Norwich. It occurred to me that Amsterdam might have been a handier location for that particular practice.

Dedicated as ever, he made it, and set about rehearsing us in concert formation. We'd chosen to have the performance and social at the rehearsal hall itself, as it would be a less formal occasion than our church-based winter and spring concerts. The SM and his team had made good use of the school's staging blocks, so that we had several stepped layers to stand on and give us good visibility, assuming we were watching the conductor. No chairs on stage, though. The plan was to sit on two facing sets of chairs at rights angles to the stage, between it and the audience, in reverse order to our singing positions, so we could process neatly onto the stage for the parts when we'd be performing, then equally neatly file off again for the in-between bits when the MD and PA played some piano duets. The SM's clear explanation made it all perfectly logical, but the height of the steps was more geared towards teenage legs than those of the average choir member, so some found it a challenge and it was frustratingly slow. Even when people were paying attention, which couldn't be guaranteed.

Never mind, we persevered, the more sprightly amongst us administering a helpful shove and heave here and there as necessary. The MD sensibly didn't labour the point but got on with the music, since there were still several tricky corners to manoeuvre in that respect too. We began to head towards some sort of polish, but the unaccustomed positions seemed to be playing havoc with concentration. All too often there was confusion as people lost their place or failed to follow an instruction that had been issued 30 seconds earlier. I could sense the MD's increasing frustration. Without thinking through what I was doing – if I had, I probably wouldn't have done it – I plonked *Madrigals and Partsongs* on the floor and strode over to the music stand. 'Excuse me', I ordered, and dismissed the MD from his podium with a flick of my hand. Up I got. Sixty-five pairs of eyes peered at me. 'Do you have any idea how far this man has travelled to get here tonight? And he has to make the same journey back again after dealing with you unruly rabble! I'm surprised he bothers. OK, the circumstances are different tonight, and the stage might not be ideal, but for goodness' sake, listen to what you're being told, and just do it! Do you want us to have a good concert, or not?' Graciously allowing the MD back into his rightful position, I resumed my place to the accompaniment of a stunned silence. One or two gave me encouraging nods, one or two even mouthed 'well done, good for you', but was there perhaps also an inaudible 'who the hell does she think she is?'

Rest, sweet nymphs... we sang, half a minute later *... let nothing affright ye ...* My notes might not have been perfect, but I seemed to have nailed the concept.

Concert day dawned bright and sunny, just as summer concert day should. This was double-edged, as a pleasant Saturday afternoon in July was such a rarity that it could seem a shame to spend it indoors rehearsing, but good weather tended to encourage our adoring public to patronise us, in the nicest possible sense. Despite my antics earlier in the week, the choir still apparently adored me, too, and thankfully gave the MD the respect and attention he deserved. They even rose to the occasion when faced with his experimental treatment of the *Waltz Scene*. 'Do you think we could include a little acting,' he asked, 'to set it in context and add some operatic atmosphere?' During the piano introduction, he wanted us to act as though we were real opera chorus members, having little *sotto voce* animated conversations with each other about what a terrific party it was. Had he suggested waltzing around the room, everyone might have dug in two left feet, but nobody seemed self-conscious about trying this background chat routine. After all, it wasn't unlike what happens on the back row at the average rehearsal anyway. We delivered the goods after a mere two minutes' warm-up. I wondered whether I should ironically suggest we get paid more for contributing this extra skill. More than zero, you understand. I thought better of it.

The summer concert didn't call for orchestra or vocal soloists, but for the *Birthday Madrigals* the piano accompaniment was supplemented by double-bass. Note for note, this was quite an expensive luxury for a 16-minute suite of songs, but it made all the difference to the finished product. The bass foundation picked out the jazz swing rhythm perfectly and lent a certain style and poise. I'd like to think Mr Rutter himself wouldn't have been ashamed of our effort, and the audience swayed and looked as though they were having fun. The show proceeded with no major hitches. Even if total accuracy eluded us, it was certainly a spirited performance, including our unpaid thespianism. The audience looked suitably entertained by the mix of our new offerings and old stalwarts, skilfully woven together by the MD as compère. *Shenandoah* had been dusted off for the occasion, prompting a revelation from my mother's considerable memory: apparently my great-grandfather, who had incidentally played the penny-whistle, hated that particular song. Thankfully, despite a brief dalliance with the recorder in junior school, I took after him in neither respect.

Everyone tucked in wholeheartedly to an impressive buffet spread after the show. *So well-planned*, the lyrics had said. In actual fact, what happened on these occasions was that, completely uncoordinated, everyone brought along a plate of bite-sized somethings, and by some miracle it was always the correct quantity, with an appropriate division of first and second courses. I could describe the taste and texture of the seductive melt-in-the-mouth savoury tartlets, the sophisticated tang of the exotic cheeses or the summer freshness of the strawberries, but what I really needed was a drink. And I don't mean sparkling water. 'A very large glass of red wine, please,' I said to the HT, who presided over a long table of beverages – bottles on a sale-or-return basis, glasses wash-up-and-return. There was one less to wash, though, as in the excitement a glass had crashed to the floor. As I stooped with a makeshift dustpan and brush made from two pieces of cardboard, someone said 'I bet this wasn't in your job description!' 'No,' I smiled, 'and I expect I'm contravening our health and safety policy too.'

It also occurred to me that I wasn't ideally clad for the task. The 'concert dress' issue had been unusually painless this time, the gents' white shirts livened up with coloured bow ties, and the ladies unanimously agreeing to long black skirts or trousers and bright blouses. I'd decided to make myself a new skirt – as if I didn't have enough to do – since the old one had seen service at ten years' worth of choir concerts and I reckoned I deserved a change. The new one was a panelled, flimsy, floaty style in which I could have played the cello – were it not for the unfortunate obstacle of not possessing that particular skill – and it splayed out around me like a composer's spilt ink as I took care of the shards. Sharp, but not as we amateur musicians know it.

And that concluded the choral year for most of us. The Committee, though, still had work to do, as the following year's activities wouldn't just happen but called for meticulous preparation. Instead of the usual rushed post-rehearsal affair at the Mermaid, we allowed ourselves a more leisurely whole evening's meeting *chez moi*, during which we managed to cover a considerable swathe of the necessary planning for rehearsals, concerts and the social side of choir life, including the visit of our French friends. A sub-group was investigating possibilities for the long weekend they'd spend with us next year, somewhat hampered by not knowing how many there would be or exactly when or how they'd get here. There was talk of coming by train rather than the usual door-to-door coach, and could we please give them details of timetables and prices for the local leg of the journey, including the cost of a coach for the day's excursion when we'd show them the delights of the British countryside? Having them all arrive by coach at a central spot to be picked up by host families was so much more convenient for us, so we set about incorporating as many obstacles as possible into our 'helpful' response, aided greatly by the exorbitant cost of the London tube.

More immediately, however, we hit upon a couple of autumn term snags. This is where the Chairman learned a bit more about the importance of keeping in touch with her team and both following up on their prompts and encouraging them to keep her informed. I'd been asked whether practice discs would need to be arranged with our usual supplier to assist us in learning Handel's *Israel in Egypt*, a tricky work with prodigious choral content. Leaving the decision until this meeting, however, turned out to be a grave error of judgment as our Man in Rome, who produces the discs, should have had much more notice and at this rate wouldn't have them ready until around half-term – by which time the 'note-bashing' stage should be well and truly over.

Problem number two: the scores. Whether to print our own from the freely downloadable version, probably more expensive than hiring, especially for a work we perhaps wouldn't perform again, or trust that we could locate sufficient hire copies in time. But the assembled gathering was fairly unanimous. I reported the discussion by phone the following day to the Librarian, who'd been absent from the meeting. 'The consensus was that we'll print them, so we can be sure everyone has the same version, plus most people like to keep their copy afterwards, so don't worry about seeking them out any more.' 'Half of them are already on their way from Stafford, and I have a load more promised from Worcester and Cardiff', came the response. So much for the Committee decision.

All was not totally lost as far as practice discs were concerned, as we were given a link to a website from which we could produce our own. It would be music only, without the helpful addition of words, but I pounced upon this life raft like a drowning Egyptian. Not quite a technophobe, I explored the link and nevertheless imagined total anarchy if we suggested individual members did it for themselves. Let's just say it was complicated. I enlisted the support of my technical adviser, the XC, who immediately got his teeth into the thrown-down gauntlet. My voyage into the World Wide Web was playing havoc with my ability to craft a well-turned metaphor. The XC came back with descriptions of biblical proportions of how he was going about the task of getting the eight different voice parts onto their respective discs. They made his musings about musical castors seem almost comprehensible. I'm sure that by the time he'd finished he wished he'd never started, as it was time-consuming and taxing in the extreme, but he hadn't bitten off more than he could chew and made a great fist of it.

Are you sitting comfortably? Then you can't be in the Sheldonian Theatre. I took a trip back to Oxford, where I lived and worked in the 1980s, as the MD was playing one of his 'professional harpsichord gigs' with the City of Oxford Orchestra. I thought it would prove an interesting contrast to his dealings with us amateurs.

Sitting amongst the dreaming spires, the Sheldonian is a domed, almost circular building, guarded by ghastly gargoyles on the perimeter fence. Inside, early evening sunshine and a hint of buildings beyond shimmered through semi-circular windows, their leaded translucence lending an illusion of underwater other-worldliness, which seemed strangely appropriate. The cherub-bedecked painted ceiling, marble-effect pillars and all manner of gilded curlicues prepared the audience for the baroque music to come. But first everyone had to be seated, and this was no mean feat. Not for the first time, revisiting old haunts, the place seemed smaller than I remembered, or shallower at least, but then all those years ago I'd been right up at the top of the building, on the backless benches. With the CC and my sister and brother-in-law in attendance, I'd shelled out for the luxury of seats with backs. In keeping with my companions for the evening, this turned out to be relative. Just half a dozen rows up from ground floor level, there were indeed narrow backs to lean against, but the

154

benches were still benches, with negligible padding. Numbness had definitely set in by Vivaldi's fourth season.

The challenge was to find ones seat in the first place, as the numbering was very subtle, and there were few gangways giving access. A maze with lots of dead ends sprang to mind. We got settled fairly early, only then to be disturbed by others in pursuit of their pew. 'That lady's very athletic', remarked an unmistakably Oxford intelligentsia voice, attached to a pair of knees which nudged my back from time to time, as another woman hopped over the seats beside us to save squeezing past. It was a health and safety officer's worst nightmare. Without dwelling on it too much, I imagined the scene 'in the unlikely event of an evacuation being necessary'. Given that we were in the hands of the professionals, maybe the musicians would carry on fiddling with dignity. Something conveying an air of panic would doubtless suit.

They weren't all on violins, of course, but with the exception of a guest oboist, the small orchestra was made up entirely of strings grouped around the harpsichord, positioned in such a way that the MD sat – on an invitingly comfy-looking stool – with his back to the majority of the audience. I shall continue to call him the MD, although in this context he wasn't the director as such, albeit the harpsichord plays a pivotal role, a foundation without which baroque music would founder. It looked a bit strange but the configuration clearly made for better communication within the orchestra, and anyway, this would feel very natural to someone who spends much of his time conducting, I supposed. Apart from him, the only other seated musician was the cellist. All the others stood throughout, not in deference to the uncomfortable audience seating but for a greater feeling of flexibility and intimacy beloved of chamber orchestras.

The MD did get to his feet and face us now and then, as his role included that of compère, announcing the pieces and introducing the soloists. That he did so with the same approachable bonhomie that he adopts in our choral concerts was no surprise, of course, because he was essentially the same musician despite the very different context. But the ambiguity of who was 'in charge' was a tricky one to fathom. The orchestra was in fact directed by the lead violinist, who presumably took the major musical and organisational decisions. The MD hinted that, had it been up to him, he would have taken a different approach, especially when it came to practising certain aspects more thoroughly. Is the corollary of this that when he is at the helm – in the context of the choir, say – some well-meaning Chairman must be careful not to rock the boat by making suggestions or querying his methods, even with the mandate of a mob of mutinous matelots? Maybe.

But enough of this self-doubt, it was time to enjoy the music. It felt strange to see the MD in action, without being part of his performing team, but I realised afresh my good fortune that I have opportunities to do just that. It was a programme of familiar works, so I helped myself to a large dollop of sheer self-indulgence, knowing I wouldn't be required to work too hard at understanding the music. I wondered how the musicians kept a freshness in their playing, when they'd doubtless played these pieces countless times before. How would you keep boredom at bay? Any job has its routine elements, I suppose, but in live music this can't be allowed to show. Apparently there was scope for a degree of improvisation at the harpsichord, which was something of a revelation as I'd considered that the exclusive domain of jazz. Entertainment was key, specifically in the key of G in the first piece, a *Concerto Grosso* by Handel. From the first joyful notes, it was clear that we could sit back and relax, as much as was possible given the furnishing deficiencies, secure in the knowledge that these eleven musicians knew what they were doing. Speaking from personal experience, Handel in the wrong hands can be a horrible hash, but this was a delight, the semiquaver runs and ornaments exquisitely executed and the subsections of the orchestra collaborating in a display of exemplary teamwork.

Teamwork of a military nature was alluded to in the introduction to the next piece. Pachelbel's *Canon* was played in memory of Lieutenant Colonel Rupert Thorneloe, shortly after his tragic death in action in Afghanistan. Members of his family in the audience shared the respectful silence as the dedication was read out, and then his favourite piece was performed, charged with added emotion.

Familiar or not, there was always something new to learn, and the programme notes taught me that the repeated two-bar foundation in the bass was called an *ostinato* – literally obstinate, persistent (the programme notes didn't go that far, but then I am the proud owner of a dictionary of musical terms, so I looked it up when I got home). Meanwhile the upper strings layered the fancy bits on top. The experience of hearing this music, with its twenty-eight variations, was magnified twenty-eight-fold by the visual impact of watching from above the three violin parts negotiate their way around the relentless canon. Seeing it somehow explained the structure of the music to me. Simply listening will never again be good enough.

While the fast movements to be found in baroque music inevitably lift the spirits, there's nothing like a fine *adagio* to tug at the heartstrings. Albinoni's *Oboe Concerto in D minor* was no exception. The programme notes got it right with 'sublime and serene'. They had me puzzled, with 'roulade-linked intervals', though, juxtaposed with dotted rhythms, which I did understand. Visions of a swiss roll, diminished due to the ministrations of my cake-loving son, swam before my eyes. The MD explained afterwards that a *roulade* is merely a *glissando*-type run of notes. Thus the wheels of my musical education keep turning.

During the interval we had the refreshment of a breath of Oxford air and a chance to flex the stiffening muscles, but we didn't bother with a drink. I wondered what would be the reaction at our choral concerts if all we offered was still or sparkling water. I didn't think I'd put it to the test.

The second half brought the most well known music of all, although I'd never before heard Vivaldi's *Four Seasons* interspersed with the complementary sonnets that appeared in the original solo violin score. The words certainly added an extra dimension and made the listener more aware of what the music was trying to say. And yet it was slightly distracting, too, and maybe the music should have been left so speak for itself, with the poetry simply printed in the programme. The music dictionary reminded me that Vivaldi had been a cleric in Venice as well as a composer, known as the Red Priest, not because of any political persuasion or choice of cassock colour, but on account of his flaming locks. I was taken back to my exposure to Roxanna Panufnik's *Tibetan Winter*. Quite a contrast, nearly 300 years apart, and yet both composers conjured up the season through shivering and skittering strings alone. Plus, in the 21st century version, that singing bowl. I wondered whether the overtones of oriental mysticism would have sat comfortably with the Red Priest.

Before I was allowed off for good behaviour for my holidays, I needed to assemble the choir's summer newsletter. This purely in-house publication was different from the termly e-newsletters and would be distributed by post, together with notification of September's AGM and a call for new Committee members, a perennial challenge. This wasn't really part of the Chairman's role, but although a little wary of setting a precedent, I'd nevertheless volunteered again as I was very familiar with compiling the newsletter since my days as Secretary and Marketing Officer. And I'm quite fond of writing. There were pictures too, and I spent an hour or so selecting from a range of photos taken at our events, bringing back (mostly) happy memories. As well as a brief round-up of the year's activities and news of what was coming up, it gave me the chance to record for posterity the valuable contribution the Committee and other helpers made to the running of the organisation. A whole paragraph was devoted to the retiring HT, who would be a tough act to follow, but thankfully the VC/PM had offered to take on financial management, a notoriously difficult position to fill. This in turn left a glaring gap in publicity (he'd also relinquish his VC title, although I hoped he didn't think he was going to escape the essential role of Chairman's confidant), but surely this would be an attractive proposition for someone else? I shouldn't have been so optimistic.

By the time I'd finished the numerous thank yous, in my mind's ear I heard the newsletter recipients chorusing 'you've thanked everybody except yourself!' Hopefully the MD's column would include something vaguely complimentary, if only 'the Chairman works bloody hard, but she's bloody hard work.' Actually, it was much nicer than that.

August
Standing room only

August brought an escape from the rat-race in the shape of my annual leave from the meetings, spreadsheets, emails and phone calls of office life. If I'd put all my callers on hold for the duration, they would have been treated to a couple of weeks of Mozart's *Eine Kleine Nachtmusik.* Given Wolfgang's prodigious output, surely the IT department could have chosen to vary this on a weekly basis and still not exhausted his repertoire, even without recourse to any other composers, but in my ten years' tenure, I can't remember it ever being different. At least climbing aboard a Ryanair flight bound for Valencia we'd surely be serenaded by something suitably Spanish, or even Irish? But no, *Eine Kleine Nachtmusik* it was. Did I mention escape?

Forget any other classical music during our holiday. No José Carreras. No *Carmen* at the swanky new opera house, a magnificent structure in glass and white mosaic, its sensual curves offering a tempting foretaste of what doubtless lay within. But unlike the super-shiny adjacent science museum, 3-D cinema and aquarium that shared the same futuristic complex and teemed with tourists, the Palau de Les Arts Reina Sofia was having a month-long siesta. Not so much as a guided tour was on offer, let alone a note of music.

I made two early discoveries: the only music I'd get in Spain would be that of the street, and plenty of it; and my knowledge of the language, even if up to scratch, which it wasn't, was going to be of limited use as the local Valencian dialect was widely used. But let's face it, even if it had been proper Castellano, my command of the lyrics would have been sketchy, although I definitely recognised the tune – strident, urgent and uninhibited.

You could even call it fugue-like, with everyone talking at once and cutting across each other. The permanent dynamic: fortissimo.

The family with whom we'd exchanged houses had described their place as a quiet village. I doubt this is ever the case (apart, perhaps from a daily 3-hour window of opportunity after lunch, when any sensible Spaniard retreats indoors to avoid the hottest part of the day) with their outdoor lifestyle, extended families and late-night eating habits. Given that our visit coincided with the local *fiesta*, ten days solid of street parades, marching bands and fireworks, not only at night-time (fair enough) but also at 8am (yes, really) and 2pm, this 'quiet village' concept struck us as a figment of their imagination.

But this street music was maybe the most authentic demonstration of what an innately musical people this is. It was natural, it was real, it was living. The processions varied in style, the Music Society – predominantly youngsters – showing considerable versatility in conjuring up the correct tone. They led the people – and an effigy of St Lawrence – through the narrow streets to the tiny church at a suitably sombre tempo, their bright orange shirts as much in contrast with the subdued rhythms as with the black-clad 'Daughters of Maria'. Old folks watched from the pavements, perched on their straight-backed chairs, olive oil aromas emanating from their open doorways.

Another evening the same musicians created the soundtrack for a parade with a totally different atmosphere. Colour, costumes, cacophony. Probably still based on some religious premise, this carnival-style occasion nevertheless seemed to be merely an excuse for a big party. Some of the more house-proud citizens had barricaded their front doors with cardboard shields, against the clouds of multi-coloured confetti that exploded from the procession from time to time. The music exploded too. Brass and percussion in particular came into their own, not so much leading as bullying the assembled masses into a frenzy of infectious excitement. Mind you, one young exhibitionist on clarinet was also determined to get her moment of fame, simultaneously dancing and playing atop a straw bale on a tractor-pulled float. An eclectic assortment of village organisations, of all ages, joined the seemingly never-ending throng either on foot or on decorated trailers. Presumably there was a theme, as efforts had been made to dress up according to your own particular group, but I couldn't fathom it out. There was everything from nursery characters to flamenco-style national dress, the latter betraying a tendency towards cross-dressing, featuring grotesque make-up and the use of over-sized balloons. The Music Society pumped out their samba rhythms with a drunken energy that threatened to go on into the early hours.

Something that would never, ever stop was the music of the sea. If you could represent this on manuscript paper (goodness knows, it's difficult enough even in words) would this be the way to capture the concept of 'refreshing' in sound? Certainly escaping to the sea-shore, capitalising on the caressing breezes, cooled and soothed the body. But more than that the dominance of the sea's song absorbed and liberated the mind from all the background noise of talking, shrieking, laughing. More illustrious souls than me have noticed this before, of course, not least Debussy and our own Vaughan Williams. The relentless tumble of the waves also put me in mind of the Bach *Solfeggietto* I was meant to be learning – once I got back home to my piano – with its rapid, rebellious runs up and down the C minor scale. The distant horizon was as flat and shiny as a Steinway, but the incoming breakers created a perpetual motion that was both visual and aural. The next wave would rear up before the previous one had subsided, the *crescendo* matched by an equal *accelerando,* but meeting headlong a *diminuendo/rallentando* combination, resulting sometimes in harmony, sometimes in discord. It was as though the sea was being directed by several different conductors. It was at once stimulating, comforting and frustrating, as it left the impression of never, ever being resolved.

While most of the choir remained in holiday mode for the whole of August, I had to keep on top of plans for the early part of the new term. Our date with the Churches Conservation Trust, staging a workshop in a draughty toilet-less church, was looming. Some delegated tasks had gone out of the stained-glass window because family crises had overtaken certain Committee members, so I found myself getting much more involved than envisaged. I was already down for collating and printing the music scores, but I also wrote detailed joining instructions and produced tickets. It was just to be hoped that there would turn out to be sufficient people to send them to. Recruitment hadn't exactly been overwhelming, even given a concerted publicity drive amongst other choirs and elsewhere. We hoped against hope that it wouldn't run at a loss. You, dear reader, may never know, as the day in question fell just outside this 'year'.

The CC may tolerate his wife's predilection for the likes of Freddie Chopin and George Freddie Handel, but his own natural inclination is for the music of Freddie Mercury. So his birthday found us at Birmingham Hippodrome for a performance of *We Will Rock You.* Not something about which I anticipated writing for this classically-bent volume, but actually, once my ears had adjusted to the pummelling, I started to realise there were some interesting parallels.

Although largely an excuse to blast out Queen's considerable repertoire, the musical did have a plot of sorts, set at a future date when all musical instruments had been banned, and people were programmed to churn out formulaic, synthesised 'music' and 'dancing'. The heroes were those with a rebellious streak and sufficient imagination and creativity to realise there has to be something more – music that comes from the heart, that has something to say – and to fight for it. Maybe in the afterlife the various Freddies are comparing notes about their respective brands of originality.

'Is this the end of the queue?' There were more people milling about further down the steps behind the Royal Albert Hall, but they didn't look as though they were consciously standing in line, as the American prommers present would have put it. 'Yes, although there should be two more people in front of you,' said a maroon-jacketed usher, handing us pink cloakroom tickets, numbered 101 and 102. The print on his lapel badge was so small that I would have had to get up close and personal to discover his name, which wouldn't have gone down too well with the Consort, so let's just call him Ranjit. 'You're allowed to leave the queue for 30 minutes if you want,' he said. As it was a typical British summers's day, we thought this quite likely, not so much for a loo- or food-break, but to dodge the threatened downpour. There was an hour or so before we could buy our £5 tickets, so time to savour the Proms atmosphere.

Black clouds went scudding across the shallow dome of the Hall, and behind us the burgundy flag of the Royal College of Music strained at its mast. From the open windows of the College came the sounds of practice

– now a soprano, now a violin – which duetted with the noise of the red Routemaster buses below. I suddenly smelled strawberries and noticed that the couple ahead of us were having a makeshift champagne picnic. The girl's flowery, backless dress suited the menu, but not the weather. Umbrellas shot up as the inevitable shower – thankfully brief – arrived. Ranjit was now patrolling the queue with a young lady usher, causing some hilarity when the brolly they were sharing collapsed on them, forcing an impromptu embrace.

A lady from North Carolina then resumed her place at number 99. Number 100 never did return, maybe deciding to opt for one of the few remaining seats instead. Some others must have given up too, as our eventual arena tickets were numbers 92 and 93. But for me, my year of living musically wouldn't be complete without the experience of being a proper prommer.

Finally there was some movement towards the famous circular building, past a posse of BBC outside broadcast vans from which spilled out a spaghetti of cables. Admitting several hundred people through one small door in the space of half an hour seemed a tall order, but the cash-only transactions were quick and we found ourselves inside and directed into the bowels of the building in no time at all. Then up through a dim stairway, emerging into the central arena, surrounded by the Hall's red and gold opulence. Impressive indeed, although strangely smaller than it appears on television. We bagged a space 'keyboard-side', a mere three or four rows back from the stage. I sat on the floor for a while, eavesdropping on the conversations of the old hands. To some, it seemed like home from home. One had almost broken even on his season ticket, having been to 32 concerts (this was Prom 57), with still a fortnight to go until the Last Night. Others tapped away on mobile phones or even laptops, or read books. I half expected somebody to take out their knitting.

The general hubbub was interrupted by a well-rehearsed sextet of prommers at the front, announcing in unison an end-of-prom collection in aid of music charities, for which £52,000 had already been raised this season. Amid the applause, someone nearby queried the timing of this speech, which traditionally was made just before the end of the interval. 'Apparently the new producer didn't want it spoiling her audience shots, so we had to do it before going live,' came the response. Authentic atmosphere? Almost, if a little manipulated.

Once on my feet again, an overheard exchange between parents and their teenagers prepared me for the first piece of music, Stravinski's ballet *Agon*. 'Do you know what the title means?' 'Is it the same as Anon?' 'No, it's like in a play, you know, as in protagonist and antagonist – it's all about the conflict.' Fair enough. Personally, I didn't worry too much about trying to decipher a story, although the discordant parts here and there bore out the theory. I simply enjoyed following the different instruments showing off, cameo-fashion, almost close enough for me to touch them. Coming across something unusual is always a bonus, and the mandolin and harp combo was a thing of beauty.

This first half-hour of performance left me with plenty of stamina to remain on foot. The main challenge with standing was having to fight the urge to move with the music, so captivating was it, and the upright stance lent a certain freedom. Now onto Tchaikovsky's *Concert Fantasia*, with a perfect view between fellow prommers' heads and over Stephen Hough's right shoulder onto his hands flying this way and that upon the Steinway. I thought it was just possible I might burst with excitement. The sheer volume and immediacy made such an impact. When a slower section at last descended, it dawned on me that I'd been holding my breath. Is that what's meant by inspirational? In contrast with the BBC Symphony Orchestra's white jackets, the pianist was all in black, even down to the handkerchief with which he mopped his brow ... and occasionally the keys too! It came as no surprise when I later read the programme – yes, I know, hardly the correct sequence of events – to learn that the second (and finial) movement included a section labelled *molto vivace* and concluded with *vivacissimo*. Vivacious with bells on. There was lots of other erudite stuff to be gleaned from the programme, and also from the commentary when I watched again online, but to me this was less the point than simply wallowing in the entertainment.

After all that we'd earned an interval sit-down and a vanilla tub, but then back to it with Steven Isserlis' interpretation of Tchaikovsky's *Variations on a Rococo Theme*. This work for cello and orchestra was also predominantly fast-paced, and by Variation 8, featuring relentless octaves, I feared the cellist's bow would end up a casualty. But at the same time the warmth and richness of the instrument – a 1726 Stradivarius – shone through, with a fine display of its impressive range. It was as if the cello sang. In humble acknowledgement of this teamwork, as Steven took the rapturous applause he inclined his cello in a bow of its own.

Tchaikovsky Night finished off with an orchestral flourish in the shape of his symphonic fantasia *Francesca da Rimini*. Dante-esque, with hell-fire and brimstone ignited by liberal use of the percussion section. This is where live music really comes into its own, as the spectacle of gong, drums and persistent cymbals feeds the eyes as well as the ears. Not to mention the emotions. The whole performance was truly uplifting. And all for a fiver!

I'd timed our visit to the capital to coincide with the first day of a series of chamber concerts at Cadogan Hall, in celebration of the 10th anniversary of Radio 3's New Generation Artists scheme. Actually, not so much a series as a marathon. Over the three-day Bank Holiday weekend there'd be twelve back-to-back performances featuring names I'd heard of from Young Musician of the Year and Cardiff Singer of the World, plus many that were new to me. The same went for the music, which ranged from the old masters to brand new commissions.

The supermarket-style offer – buy three, get one free – was too good to miss, so once again we queued up early for our tickets and looked forward to a whole day's entertainment for £15. Last night's acquaintance from North Carolina emerged from the box office triumphantly brandishing her wodge of tickets, and it occurred to me that by the end of the day we could be best friends with some of these people.

The cheap and cheerful tickets gave us admission to the gallery upstairs (up lots and lots of stairs, incidentally) where, luxury of luxuries, we got to sit down. I was expecting uncomfortable benches, but they were pews with full wooden backs and plentiful padding. Plenty of legroom for the CC, too, as well as space for my notebook.

The handsome clean white exterior of the Hall was echoed inside. It was bright and welcoming, with sunlight spilling through the leaded windows, mostly clear but edged with pale green borders. In the stairwells and other public spaces, the stained glass was more elaborate. The tall cappuccino curtains matched the colour of the shell motifs around the edge of the gallery, subtle against the white paint. The stage was set simply for a string quartet ... and the requisite paraphernalia for live radio transmission.

The low buzz of conversation abated with the presenter's arrival on stage. But just before we went on air, she explained that we should in fact keep up the animated chat, in the right places, to convey the appropriate 'live Radio 3 atmosphere'. We were given signals to follow, indicating when to cease the applause and when to start it up again. All in all, it gave the sense of not just witnessing the music-making, but actively participating. Back at home the following day, I tuned in to an explanation of Van Bree's *Allegro for Four String Quartets*, the presenter getting the audience to demonstrate something of its structure by means of a Mexican wave. I'm not sure that worked terribly well on radio, but having been there the day before, I was in with a chance of picturing it.

Being there in person once again proved the value of live music. The sheer physicality – let alone the sound – was something not to be missed. My notebook started filling up with details of how this violinist would rise bodily from her chair with the rise of the melody, that violist would shoot out his legs theatrically with each *sforzando,* and how the cellist from the Kungsbacka Piano Trio shuffled in on crutches and acknowledged the applause half-kneeling on his stool.

Particularly visual was Alexander Goehr's *Since Brass, nor Stone...*, percussionist Colin Currie joining the Pavel Haas Quartet and laying into his 'battery of bangy things', as the presenter chose to call it. Exciting stuff. During a brief lunch break in the King's Road sunshine, a young American who taught music in London confided that she was planning to turn that into a 'does melody matter?' exercise for her pupils. Lorraine was envious that we'd been to the Prom the night before, as she was a fan of Steven Isserlis. 'Actually, believe it or not, I once taught his son cello! Steven turned up early to collect him and chose to sit in while I finished the lesson. Can you imagine how nerve-racking that was! At the end he said "So, is the cello your first instrument?" "No, I'm a violinist," I admitted, and his relief was visible!'

To write a blow by blow account of the whole day's music-making would take until the NGA's next birthday party. But speaking of blows, wind quintet The Galliard Ensemble joined forces with the Aaronowitz Ensemble to play Spohr's *Nonet in F major*. This was a novelty in more ways than one, as I'd never even heard of Spohr nor had I ever knowingly heard a nonet, familiar though I was with everything from a solo to an octet. This was engaging music, control passing between the woodwind and strings by turns, and emphasising the team playing inherent in chamber music.

Other highlights emerged from the final concert of the day. Natalie Clein and Tom Poster appeared to have eyes in the backs of their heads, such was the sense of telepathy between cello and piano in Delius' *Cello Sonata*. Come to think of it, why don't they sit where they can see each other better? Jennifer Pike accompanied tenor Andrew Kennedy in a selection of Holst songs, modest in this uncharacteristic supporting role and pointing out that the violin imitates the voice anyway. The musicians all displayed a real understanding of working together, one big mutual appreciation society.

Jennifer got her moment in the spotlight in any case, rounding off the day with Elgar's *Violin Sonata*. After the hectic schedule of the proceedings and some unfamiliar music to grapple with, it was like being wrapped in a security blanket.

September again
Handel with care

If anyone in the choir was experiencing withdrawal symptoms because of the summer break, they quickly snapped out of them when we plunged headlong into a first run-through of *Israel in Egypt*. If anyone was itching to learn something challenging, now was their chance. What a lot of notes! What a lot of words! We sang from scratch about plagues of flies, lice and locusts, and was Handel perhaps the only composer ever to set the word 'nostrils' to music? Diction was obviously going to be paramount if we stood a chance of bringing this drama to life. And a miracle with the music wouldn't go amiss, either.

When it was time for me to make some half-time announcements, everyone looked a bit battered by their adventures in the Red Sea, and I hoped we wouldn't be in for a mass exodus. Assuming my best start-of-term enthusiasm, I hopped onto the podium like an escapee from a plague of frogs and croaked, 'Great to be back singing again, isn't it!' Glazed looks all round, as though shell-shocked. 'Isn't it?' this time with a question mark.

Symmetry is a very pleasing tool in many art forms. There's something rather satisfying about its predictability and balance. It offers reassurance. It lends a sense of completeness. Not least in music, from the simplest up-and-down scale or arpeggio to the full-blown symphony with bookend motifs, various volumes and dividers nestling in between. As for this volume, when I began I knew that my musical year in print would start and finish with the choir's Annual General Meetings, but I've experienced other symmetries too.

171

Twelve months on, I paid a return visit to Symphony Hall for the launch of Andris Nelsons' second year at the helm of the City of Birmingham Symphony Orchestra. His had been a year, not so much of living, but of triumphing musically, and he'd already had his contract doubled from the original three-year term. Just so long as the choir didn't get any similar ideas about me.

The concert was entitled *The Perfect Fifth,* referring to Beethoven's famous symphony, but of course the play on words reminded me of my theory exam which had tidily occupied the mid-point of my year. Andris first took up not the baton but a microphone, and talked to the full house about the structure of the evening's programme. Starting in C major for Wagner's Prelude to *The Maestersingers,* it would come full circle, via Brahms' *Piano Concerto Number 2,* to Beethoven's *Fifth*, which kicks off in C minor but concludes triumphantly back at C major – the foundation of all music, as Andris pointed out. Would I remain as grounded at the end of my year, or would the ups and downs have knocked me off my feet? Or, to put it another way, instead of depicting life's rich tapestry, would I have made an asymmetrical Jackson Pollock of it?

The Consort and I had a fabulous view of the Maestro, as we sat close to the stage but sideways-on. It was mesmerising to see him switch the baton from right hand to left. Every time he turned to the violins we got the full force of his facial expressions which were, well, expressive. 'I am a Wagner fan, and I'm going to make you one too,' proclaimed his irrepressible smile. He could have coaxed beautiful music from the most reluctant players – which these weren't – and when it came to a string passage in the second movement of the Brahms, he created the illusion of personally playing all

172

the instruments simultaneously. Such poise, precision, passion, connection.

As for solo-playing, rather than the Russian at the ivories, it was Eduardo Vassallo who stole the show in the piano concerto's slow movement, his cello singing a heart-melting melody. I could have listened to that all night and had a little taste of it again in a half-time honey and ginger ice cream. But it was time for stirring stuff in Beethoven's *Fifth*, which is so much more than those first four famous notes. Predominantly majestic and exciting, it gave the musicians quite a work-out, and the dark hair that fell over Andris' collar began to prove that genius is significantly more indebted to perspiration than inspiration. There were nevertheless dreamy passages of calm, too, Andris stooping down low to control the quietest section. He held the orchestra not so much in the palm of his hand as in his heart.

They didn't always do as they were told, however. As a direct parallel with September Marque I, this concert found Andris forced to acknowledge the applause for himself, the leader obstinately refusing to stand the orchestra when bidden to share it. I wondered whether the choir could try that, to show our respect for the MD. Chances are that one lone soul would be totally oblivious to the planned affectionate mutiny and for the first time ever would be aware of and respond to the MD's gesture, while the rest of us resolutely declined to budge. Best leave such theatricality to the professionals.

Standing or sitting, we choral singers tended to be creatures of habit, occupying the same position week by week. But the MD had a new idea up his turned-back sleeves. To add to the complexity, *Israel in Egypt* was a work for double choir, calling for harmony not merely across the sections but also within each voice type. Instead of our usual left-to-right soprano, tenor, bass and alto blocks, with firsts and seconds in each block as necessary, he wanted to be faced with Choir 1 (sops, altos, tenors, basses) to his left and Choir 2 mirroring them to his right. We were grouped lozenge-fashion (throat lozenge, perhaps?) around him, such that we sopranos on the two extremities effectively faced each other. And effective it was. It meant we heard each other better and were more conscious of the desired harmonies. Thus I found myself on the opposite side of the room from usual, which was fine as a change is as good as a rest. And I certainly couldn't see myself getting one of those, apart from the squiggles in amongst the crotchets and quavers, for quite some time to come.

I quickly realised that my usual method of absorbing the music, repeatedly playing the practice disc on my commute to work, wasn't going to be enough with such complex music. What it required was a more multi-sensory experience, which in this case turned out to involve taste as well. I took to spending my lunch hours back in the car park so I could listen again in splendid isolation, carefully following the score propped up on the steering wheel while tucking into my cheese and tomato sandwiches. Manna was off. Gradually the notes and rhythms required to depict the beleaguered Israelites' adventures sank in, just like the Egyptians and their horses into the miraculous sea. It was worth it even if the car ended up rather crumby. The worst that could happen would be a plague of ants. They'd be no match for the locusts, though, which 'devoured the fruits of the ground', a phrase that demanded to be sung 'with relish'.

Pushed for time as we were, the MD still threw in the odd music theory lesson for our edification, sparked off by the work in hand. Thus we learned that spreading a single syllable over several notes, as in hailstones that 'ra-a-a-a-an a-lo-o-ng the ground' is termed melismatic. If only I'd known that when tackling those

174

melody compositions for the theory exam. Some of it seemed blatant fiction though; can entries really be 'arpeggiated'? Surely musicians aren't allowed to make up words: that's the preserve of writers? What was certain was that our overlapping entries had to be treated with extreme care. Over and over again we sang 'the horse and his rider hath He thrown into the sea', and there was many a false start when the horse set off too early. Imagine runaway wild steeds, and you come close to the chaos of those first gallops through that movement, although we lived in hope of reaching the finishing post intact. Time would tell. Time outside the limits of this particular volume.

There was no escape from Handel. Minding my own business in the kitchen one afternoon, I was busy baking with Radio 3 keeping me company. A Handel *Chaconne* turned out to be the perfect stimulus for stirring the sultana cake, as well as the imagination. It was so fast and furious that by the end I had visions of the harpsichord bursting into flames; hence the expression 'if you can't stand the heat, stay out of Baroque music'. The cake turned out very well, incidentally, vindicating the CC for a domestic error. 'Is there a reason for buying this big bag of sultanas?' I'd asked, as I put away the shopping. 'It was on your list', he replied indignantly. After a minute's puzzlement, light dawned. 'That said satsumas!' The two fruits have now become interchangeable in our household.

As my year of living musically drew to a close, anybody with a slightly more balanced lifestyle might surmise that I'd packed so much into it that it would be enough to put me off music for good. Far from it. Music had become as vital to me as breathing in and out. And anyway, there'd be a further two years of my chairmanship to survive for a start. My bright ideas for the choir didn't show much sign of abating, although I approached them with a little more realism these days. I counted it a success if we got through the run-of-the-mill stuff without too many hitches. Innovations may take a little longer, but they'd come. I wasn't about to give up my own private music-making either. Having satisfied myself and the Associated Board that I understood enough about music theory to open the doors to another piano exam, why not give it a bash? 'Nerves' is the obvious cautionary riposte, but maybe I'm just a glutton for punishment. A return visit to Jackdaws beckoned in the new year, for some intensive piano tuition. I'd be going up in the world if I was allowed to actually play the Steinway rather than merely dust it. Funds and time permitting, I'd also like to revisit the scenes of many of the other highlights of my musical year: Spring Sounds, the Proms, and concerts and workshops various, not to mention a whole world of tempting events and venues that hadn't yet had a look-in.

I even contemplated a belated career change. Not as a musician, I hasten to add, I'm not that self-deluding. But when a management post came up at a symphony orchestra that's no stranger to these pages, I thought I'd have a go. I might not fit the profile of their typical employee, but with my all-round experience and above all my passion for making live music happen, I reckoned I had something to offer and was in with a chance. 'That was quick!' I exclaimed to the CC, when I opened a rejection letter on my return from work one Friday evening. 'The closing date was only today ... no, wait a minute, they're turning me down for something I haven't even applied for!' Jumping to the logical conclusion that my application hadn't made it into the right short-listing meeting, I immediately phoned up, to be told the relevant person had already left the office. So I sent an email politely pointing out the error and asking for reassurance, not expecting an answer until Monday. But an apologetic message mid-evening was followed at 11.00pm by further news that I wasn't to be invited for interview for the correct job either. If I was left with the bitter taste of having been treated unfairly, I consoled myself that if that's how the professionals operate, I'm better off with the amateurs anyway. I lived to revisit that opinion at our post-AGM Committee meeting, but that, dear reader – yes, you guessed it – falls into another year.

The next hurdle fast approaching was the AGM, so if I was to stay in the saddle I'd have to prove I had a firm grip on the reins. Maybe choir uniforms should now include hard hats. There wasn't likely to be a rush of opposition candidates, though, just as there hadn't been twelve months earlier, and indeed the difficulty lay in press-ganging sufficient people to occupy vacancies. Being voluntary in nature, you can't force anyone to take them on. Bringing to fruition our fixed-term-of-office policy would probably require a miracle of Red Sea proportions.

I'd had plans to liven up the necessarily rather dull routine of an AGM by asking the MD to play something motivational for us by way of introduction as people were gathering, but as the meeting was tagged onto the end of a rehearsal there was no time for such civilization. However, if everyone was expecting the usual businesslike Chairman's Report, they didn't get it. What it gave me was the chance to round up and reflect on the ups and downs of a year which had absorbed so much of my energy and creativity, but which on balance seemed far from disastrous. I stood up and took a deep breath.

Since this scenario allows me to make a spokesperson's soliloquy, I'm shamelessly sneaking in a significant sprinkling of 'S' words, compensating for the fact that the slithery consonant must be severely subdued in singing sessions. - Polite giggles all round, and a wry smile from the MD. OK, I'd captured their attention.

Skirting around the fact that the superior voice part starts with an 'S', - indignant sniggers from everyone apart from the sopranos – *let's begin with the obvious:*

Singing*: We seem to be going from strength to strength, and have had a stupendous year, being stretched into new territory as well as enjoying some of our old favourites. Conscious of the swathes of solo work in some of the repertoire, though, we asked for works that are satisfyingly choral, and we've certainly been served that in this term's Israel in Egypt. Our part of the bargain is to make sure we put in some serious score-scrutiny and learn it well. Even with more familiar territory, whether secular or sacred, there's always been something new to learn and new ways to bring the music alive. Inspired programming – I'm thinking particularly of the Vaughan Williams-themed Christmas concerts – has given our audiences something scintillating.*

Social*: The social side of the choir is not to be sneezed at, and as well as the enjoyment of mixing together vocally week by week, this year has given us many opportunities, including garden parties, a barn dance, a quiz and our summer concert social, to simply enjoy each other's company. People matter. People matter in terms of getting the job done, too, and I'd like to record our debt to those on and around the Committee for all the hard work that goes on behind the scenes. They're a splendid bunch.* – With a bit of luck that might encourage others to get on board.

Sadness*: There have been sad times too, though. One of the toughest aspects of my role has been to let*

178

everyone know, on too many occasions, of bereavements that our members have suffered. *Others have had illnesses or personal struggles to cope with. Hopefully the solidarity we share with one another has offered some small comfort, as has the power of music itself.* – That was certainly true for me when faced with organisational niggles, and the sage nods around the room seemed to endorse the sentiments.

Strangers*: So much for all of us who make up our Society. We've had strangers amongst us too, including some lovely new members and lovely new soloists. And who could forget the massed voices when we joined forces with The Other Choir for our exciting performance of The Creation?* – Who indeed? – *They were interesting, challenging and even stressful times, but a dedicated Committee, strong musical leadership and the unifying factor of the music made it a success, even though we afterwards voted to remain as a single Society rather than amalgamate permanently.*

John Rutter's music was no stranger to us, but to have the composer visit us in person in the summer and rehearse the Birthday Madrigals with us was very special indeed – an occasion in its own right, and something that gave an extra edge to our concert.

There'll be another opportunity to welcome strangers shortly, when we put on our day workshop next month – a different sort of venture which we hope, with your help, will be a big success. – I tried to keep the panic out of my voice, as recruitment had been dangerously low and at worst we'd go into the red.

Then looking further ahead, the French invasion. Lots of our colleagues from our exchange choir are already well known to many of us, of course, but doubtless there'll be new faces on both sides of La Manche. We'll be asking for help with hospitality, and please get involved with our musical and social

179

programme, which will include a day trip and soirée on the Friday, with the main musical focus and concert on the Saturday. It promises to be a superb and enriching experience.

The Standard Stuff*: Our standard programme meanwhile will no doubt keep us busy and fulfilled during the coming year, and let's hope we can make sublime sounds and remain serene and solvent!* – Complicit chuckles from the outgoing and incoming Treasurers – *I searched for an 'S' word that would express the pride I feel in our choir, but could only come up with 'smug',* - snorts and even a few guffaws – *which isn't quite right. Instead, I'll spur us on with this: as we sally forth into another year, let's strive for a successful season's serenading!*

It was hardly Martin Luther-King, but they liked it, applauded and even looked mildly motivated. On the front row of the tenors, VP Pat, who could always be relied upon to put in a good word for the Chairman, spontaneously gave a vote of thanks. 'You hit the ground running when voted in and you haven't stopped since!' Not fast enough, perhaps, though, as I still had to run the gauntlet of 'Any Other Business' at the close of the meeting. I could almost have written the script for this episode in advance, as you could always guarantee questions from one or two particular members, who would find something impertinent, intrusive or downright perplexing to raise. This in answer to my request for someone to take on the marketing vacancy: 'Why is it so important to have yet more publicity? What's the point of employing someone?' Employing someone! Whoever mentioned employing someone? Remuneration for Committee members, now there's an original idea. Several of my fellow unpaid volunteers congratulated me on politely, firmly and (almost) unflappably taking the meeting in my stride. A message from the MD the following day was similarly encouraging. He hoped I hadn't been discombobulated by the more bizarre remarks. I spent five minutes wallowing in the novelty of receiving an email featuring the word 'discombobulated' and then reassured him that, convinced of the backing of an overwhelming majority, I rather felt emboldened. If not yet powerful enough to have appointed a Publicity Manager. Maybe next year.

Any other business
Who's who

CC   Chairman's Consort
CM   Concert Manager
GB   Go Betweens
HS   Honorary Secretary
HT   Honorary Treasurer
MD   Musical Director
PA   Piano Accompanist
PE   Publicity Expert
PM   Publicity Manager
PT   Piano Teacher
SM   Stage Manager
VC   Vice Chairman
VP   Vice President
XC   Ex Chairman